*"Were you beaten as a child?"
Shanni asked—and waited.*

"Yes," Nick said harshly.

"Nick—"

"Don't you dare feel sorry for me. If I'm not over it now I never will be."

"I don't think you can ever be over something like that. Kids can bounce back from a hard time—but if they don't think they're loved...."

"Harry will be okay."

She hadn't been talking about Harry—but now she turned to look down at the sleeping little boy.

"I guess." She smiled and turned back to Nick. "If you stay on his side...."

"Hey, I'm committing myself to nothing here."

"You're already committed."

Families in the Making!

In the orphanage of a small Australian seaside town called
Bay Beach are little children desperately in need of love.
Some of them have no parents, some are simply
unwanted—but each child dreams about having
their own family someday....

The answer to their dreams can also be found in
Bay Beach! Couples who are destined for each other—
even if they don't know it yet—are brought together by love
for these tiny children. Can they find true love
themselves—and finally become a real family?

Look out for the next PARENTS WANTED story:
Their Baby Bargain
by Marion Lennox
July 2001, #3662

A CHILD IN NEED

Marion Lennox

PARENTS
WANTED

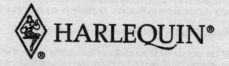

HARLEQUIN®

TORONTO • NEW YORK • LONDON
AMSTERDAM • PARIS • SYDNEY • HAMBURG
STOCKHOLM • ATHENS • TOKYO • MILAN • MADRID
PRAGUE • WARSAW • BUDAPEST • AUCKLAND

ISBN 0-373-03650-7

A CHILD IN NEED

First North American Publication 2001.

PROLOGUE

'MY PERFECT woman…'

'Yeah, Nick. You must have *someone* pictured in that cool, calculating head of yours. If you were ever to consider marriage…'

'Ha!'

'No, but say your career depended on it. Say you really needed a wife. Who would it be?' Nick's fellow lawyers were clustered around the bar late on Friday night, and they weren't letting him off the hook.

So Nick thought about it—but just to humour them. There was no way this could ever be serious.

'Okay. Wife requirements coming up.' He frowned. 'Anyone I married would have to be independent. I don't need a wife so she couldn't need a husband.'

There was a hoot of derisive laughter and the questioning intensified. 'We guessed that much. Independent. Okay. What else?'

'Beats me.' Nick gave a mental shrug. This was stupid. Marriage wasn't on his cards at all. But if it was…

'She'd have to be really something,' he said slowly, thinking it through. 'Tall and gorgeous. Of course.'

'Oh, of course,' his friends agreed, rolling their eyes. 'Cat-walk gorgeous.'

'Trophy-wife gorgeous,' Nick agreed. 'After all, that's the only reason I'd be marrying.'

'And smart?'

'Absolutely. Professional something. A lawyer or a doctor, maybe. So she'd have her own life.'

'Rich?'

'Yep. There's no chance I'm supporting any woman!'

'That's a bit unfair. You make a mint.'

'And that's the way I like it. Wealth. Position. Travel. What else is there in life?'

'How about kids?' they asked curiously.

'You have to be joking!' That was emphatic. 'No!'

'Now, how did we guess that?' His friends now had their summary. 'So... Gorgeous. Intelligent. Rich. Independent. Wanting no ties. Cold as ice? Something like you, in fact?'

'Am I cold?' Nick asked mildly, but he knew the answer. Of course he was cold. Nick Daniels kept his emotions to himself. He didn't get involved. Not after what he'd been through.

So this conversation was ridiculous. Marriage for Nicholas Daniels was never going to happen.

'It must be getting close now—or has John popped the question already?'

Shanni McDonald laughed and shrugged. They were a strange partnership, these two. Shanni, kindergarten director at twenty-seven, still looked about sixteen. Her assistant, Marg, was in her fifties, but they worked together brilliantly. There was only one disadvantage as far as Shanni was concerned. Marg's age meant she was never backward in asking the hard questions.

So now she was waiting for an answer, and there was only one to give.

'Not yet.'

'He will. I can feel it. And you'll agree. 'Cos he has to be your perfect man.'

'I guess.'

'Isn't he just what you've always wanted?' Marg demanded. 'Don't you have a list?' She held up one finger after another. 'Lives locally and never wants to move. Loves animals and kids. Family man. Loves the country.

Has room to stable horses and house half a dozen kids. Your families like each other. Everything's right, then. John fits everything on the list.'

'I guess he does,' Shanni said, and tried to stop the note of doubt creeping into her voice.

But Marg was astute enough to hear it. 'So what's wrong?'

Shanni caught herself and shrugged. 'Nothing, I guess… When he pops the question I'll be the happiest girl in the world. After all, he *is* my perfect match. Where could I find a better partner in life than John?'

CHAPTER ONE

THE man who just might interfere with her wedding plans
wasn't talking marriage now. Nick had other things on his
mind, all bleaker than the thought of an unwanted wife.

'I don't want to be a magistrate in Hicksville. I don't
wish to be within a hundred miles of this place—so why
on earth am I here?'

It was a good question, but there were sensible answers.
Nick Daniels had one burning ambition and one only—to
make high-court judge. Historically, once a lawyer joined
Queens Counsel he could be appointed a judge without
leaving the city, but that was hard to do now. There were
new rules. No one wanted the country magistrate positions,
and there was only one way to force aspiring judges to take
them on.

'If you want the plum job, then you need to do the hard
work first,' Nick had been told by the head of his chambers.
'Politically there's no other way. There's a job going as
local magistrate at Bay Beach. Great little fishing town,
four hours' drive from Melbourne. You're not married—
you've no kids—no ties to keep you in town. Put in the
hard work there, boy, and we'll see what we can do.'

'For how long?' Nick had been aghast.

'Two years.'

'Two *years*!'

'You never know.' Abe Barry had sucked his pipe and
had surveyed his hawk-like junior with the beginnings of
amusement. Nick was too darned clever by half. If he didn't
get shot of him soon Nick would be edging him aside as
chamber head before he knew it. 'You might even enjoy a

spot of rustic idyll. You could apply for a county court judge position and stay there for life!'

'In your dreams!'

'No. In *your* dreams, and I know you dream of the big one,' Abe had told him, the steel in his voice telling Nick he had no choice in this. 'But there's only one way to get it. You've had a taste of magistrate work already so you know the ropes. Now take yourself off to the country and show us what you're made of.'

'What I'm made of...' Nick's hands clenched the wheel of his sleek little sports car until his knuckles showed white. Magistrate at Bay Beach! It was an uninspiring name for an uninspiring place. Nightmare stuff.

Accustomed to big-time criminal cases, now he'd be dealing with parking infringements, fines for illegal fishing and not much else. Though it served as a base for a much larger fishing and farming community, Bay Beach township had less than a thousand inhabitants.

So...fishing and farms! What qualifications did he have for judging farming or fishing disputes? What did he know of either?

Farms gave milk, steak, or wool which was exported to Italy and returned as Nick's superbly tailored suits. And fishing... Fishing produced salmon and caviar. That was the end of Nick's interest in farming and in fishing. Period.

Two years as country magistrate... Two years of purgatory! He rounded the headland, still groaning. Bay Beach lay before him, its whitewashed stone cottages glistening in the morning sun. The fishing fleet was coming in—at least, it must be the fishing fleet. There were six boats heading into harbour, and surely there couldn't be many more boats than six in this ends-of-the-earth place?

'I'll go stark, staring crazy,' he told himself. The sea air was blowing warmly on his face but he hardly noticed. His skin was so tanned he didn't fuss about protection, and his deep black hair was combed into submission so firmly the sea air didn't shift it. He sniffed—and wrinkled his aquiline nose in disgust. Salt! And cow dung! Ugh! Give him petrol fumes and city pollution any day!

Another bend in the road and the town limits came into view. There was a petrol station on this side of the town boundary and, on impulse, Nick pulled in. He had to fill the car with petrol, and he might as well do it now—give him a few more minutes before he entered this dump!

He pulled up to the bowser, looked idly over at the youth pulling petrol at the pump beside him—and his life changed for ever.

'I need to go to the bathroom.'

Shanni sighed and rolled her eyes as three-year-old Hugh made his life or death announcement. It was Friday morning—thank heaven—the end of a week which seemed to have gone on for ever.

'Marg, can you take Hugh?' Her assistant at Bay Beach Kindergarten was preparing milk and fruit. This would be Marg's fourth trip to the toilet during reading, and the way they were going milk and fruit wouldn't be ready until lunch-time. But needs must.

Calm and unflappable, Marg grinned good-naturedly, shrugged, and took Hugh's hand. 'Okay, Hugh, let's go. But we'd best hurry. This is a very exciting story.'

'Miss McDonald always tells exciting stories,' Hugh announced. 'I tell them to my dad, and my dad says, "Why can't exciting things like that happen around here?"'

'I guess pirates wouldn't be a very peaceful thing to have around in real life,' Shanni said thoughtfully. 'What do you think, boys and girls? Would we like it if a real live pirate climbed through the window?'

'Oh-h-h no...'

But as Shanni went back to reading she couldn't stop a vague feeling of regret. *Oh-h-h, no.* But…

Maybe not a pirate—but something! Sometimes Bay Beach was just too quiet for words.

I wouldn't mind one very small pirate, she thought as she went back to reading of *Dirty Dick's Dastardly Deeds*. An image of her John rose before her—kind and placid and as immovable as the Friesian cows he ran on his property. They'd be married soon, Shanni knew. All in good time. When he'd paid off the new dairy and had enough to put a decent size down payment on a new home. He had it all planned out.

'Just a very small pirate,' she whispered to herself, and then went back to her book—which was the only place around here that things happened.

It was Len Harris.

Nick stared at the youth beside him and the name was burned into his brain. They were all of two feet apart. No!

Two weeks back, Nick's junior, Elsbeth, had taken Len on as a duty solicitor case, and she'd asked Nick's advice. 'He's on his ninth conviction but he's only sixteen. How do I keep him out of remand home?'

'You don't,' Nick said, skimming through the file and closing it with a snap of finality. 'Hopeless. Save your talent for something worthwhile.'

'He probably won't even get to court,' Elsbeth said morosely. 'I'll spend days on this and then he'll skip bail.'

Which was exactly what must have happened. Nick had seen him in his pre-court briefing. Len had been dragged into chambers by his social worker and, like Elsbeth, Nick had thought the kid's chances of making court were somewhere between zero and none. Len had looked surly, defiant and fearless.

Which was just the look he gave Nick now. The youth

stared at him for a long minute—enough to recognise Nick
as surely as Nick recognised him—and then he swore. He
threw the fuel hose aside so it snaked away still spurting
petrol, he leaped into the Mercedes he was driving—that
had to be stolen—and he spun out of the petrol station
leaving a trail of burned rubber behind him.

'Harry, don't you want to hear about the pirates?' Before
she returned to reading, Shanni tried one more time to at-
tract Harry's attention. Harry was three years old—almost
four—like the rest of her class—but Harry was different.
Abused and battered, he'd only just joined the kindergarten
after being moved from an uncaring family situation into
one of the five homes that made up the local orphanage.

'You don't need to take him on if you don't think you
can cope,' Shanni had been told by the welfare authorities.
But of course she'd taken him. How could she not? Harry
was enough to wrench the most hardened of hearts.

Harry's leg was recovering now from a break which had
been poorly tended in the past. It had needed resetting, and
because the healing was taking so long it was bound in a
fibreglass cast with an inbuilt heel. The whole structure
seemed much too heavy for such a little body.

The child was so small—little more than a baby, really—
and he was permanently withdrawn from the world. He
spent his kindergarten time underneath the furthest table,
and if Shanni or anyone else tried to drag him out he kicked
and screamed until he was allowed to return. After a month
in kindergarten, Shanni was no closer to reaching him than
the day he'd arrived.

But still she tried.

'This is a really exciting book,' she told Harry, but the
huge eyes peering out distrustfully at the world edged further back into the shadows.

The rest of her children were waiting. Shanni sighed and kept on reading. Pirates. Pirates and problems...

'Police? It's Nick Daniels here, the new magistrate.' Nick was back behind the wheel of his car and was barking into his mobile phone. 'There's a youth driving south into town in a grey Mercedes. He's sixteen, a bail absconder and erratic as hell. He's seen me and thinks I'm after him. The way he's driving he's heading for trouble. I'm driving behind him, but I've backed off so he doesn't think I'm chasing him. He's turning left toward the coast. He's... *No!*'

Shanni read on.

> *He took his cutlass in his hand and waved it fiercely over his head. "Give me all your treasure," the pirate yelled, and Miss Mary frowned.*
> *"You're not a very polite pirate. Hasn't your mummy ever taught you to say please?"*
> *Dirty Dick glowered and waved his cutlass some more. "All your treasure, I said—"'*

There was an almighty smash, and a huge grey car came crashing through the kindergarten fence. Shanni's book dropped to the floor as the car ended up with its nose pressed hard against the kindergarten windows.

'It's crashed.' Nick was still connected to the police, his hands-free phone letting him concentrate on driving as he talked. 'Dear God, it's a kindergarten. I'm pulling up. Back off. Don't let any police near. He's capable of doing something really stupid...'

But even as he said it he heard sirens in the distance and knew it was too late. Len, sitting dazed and scared witless in his smashed car, would hear the sirens too. If he was capable of getting out of the car, what would he do now?

And suddenly Nick knew. He swerved into the kerb, got out, left his car where it was and started to run.

'Children, don't move. Marg, stay with them.' Marg had burst back into the room at the sound of the crash and was staring out through the cracked windows at the mess outside. Her jaw was sagging almost to her waist. 'Call the ambulance and the police.' Shanni could see smoke drifting up from the engine. If the driver was trapped...

She moved fast toward the door—and then stopped dead.

A boy was climbing from the wreck. He looked about fifteen—skinny and undergrown, filthy windcheater, ripped jeans, long fair hair that hung down over his eyes. He had a cut on his forehead and he staggered as he took his first step.

Shanni opened the door—and then saw what he was holding. As she saw him, he saw her. And raised his hand.

A gun was levelled straight at her heart.

'What the...?' Her words were barely uttered before she was interrupted.

'Don't move. Don't do anything stupid.' It wasn't the boy. It was a man's voice, tough and authoritative. Shanni, her hand still on the door and standing as if she was frozen, looked beyond the boy and saw a man behind the smashed Mercedes.

He couldn't be more different from the boy. He was in his thirties, immaculately dressed in smart casual trousers, a linen short-sleeved shirt and a tie that must have set him back a kindergarten teacher's weekly salary. He was olive-skinned, dark-eyed, and tall—six foot or so to Shanni's five-four. His jet-black hair was combed back in city-sophisticate style, and his bone structure was strong and...and male, for want of a better word. *Very* male.

In short he looked a man accustomed to strength and accustomed to command. His deep brown eyes were creased against the sun, and his words were sharp, incisive and they flicked like a whip.

'Len, don't do anything stupid. You're hurt. Put the gun down and let us help.'

'You…' The boy's breath hissed in as he wheeled to face him, and his fear was palpable. 'You were going to put me away. You and that stupid other lawyer. Well, no chance. I'm not going to remand school.' He waved the gun back at Shanni, and his hand trembled. 'Get inside.' Then he turned and waved it at Nick. 'You, too. You try anything and the lady gets it.'

His hand wasn't trembling enough. The gun was too steady to do anything else.

There was nothing for it but to obey.

So in the kindergarten there were now twenty-five goggle-eyed children, one goggle-eyed kindergarten assistant, Len and Shanni and Nick.

'Line…line up against the wall.' Len sounded desperately unsure. The sirens in the distance were getting closer. 'Everyone.'

'Leave the children on the mat,' Shanni said, in a voice that made Nick take a closer look at her. No fainting or hysterics here, then. Shanni was diminutive, far shorter than Nick, with shoulder-length blonde curls running riot, blue eyes and freckles. She was wearing jeans and an oversized man's shirt smeared with finger paints. She looked about sixteen, but her voice was authoritative and as sure as an experienced school-marm.

'We'll sit on the mat with the children,' she told him. 'Then you can point the gun at all of us and the children won't be frightened.'

Len took an audible breath. He really was a child himself. 'O...kay.' The gun waved wildly. Outside a siren cut off, and there was the sound of running feet. 'You...' He waved the gun at Nick. 'Stand just outside the door. Tell them...'

'Tell them what?' Nick, too, sounded calm, much calmer than he was feeling. Fear and guns and tiny children. This had all the makings of a nightmare.

'Tell them not to come in or I'll kill someone.'

'I'll go...' He took a step toward the door.

'No!' Len was indecisive and terrified, changing his mind in the instant.

'If you want me to give them a message fast, then I need to go outside,' Nick said calmly. 'I can't tell them anything from in here.'

'I'll kill the kids if they come in!'

'I understand, but I need to go outside to tell them that. Now, or they're coming in.' He cast a swift glance at Shanni, hoping desperately there were some brains behind the riot of blonde curls. Then he looked back at Len, forcing his voice to sound calm as he spoke to him. 'If you stay behind me, you can keep the gun trained on me while I speak.'

'I...'

'They're coming in, Len.'

'No!' The boy was clearly frightened half to death. He waved the gun at the room in general. The children were stunned into absolute silence and Shanni had sunk down onto the mat beside them.

And Len made up his mind. 'Go out,' he ordered Nick. Tell them what I said. But I'm behind you. The rest of you...don't move or I'll kill him.'

And he shoved the gun into Nick's back and pushed him out the door.

There were sirens screaming from everywhere. How many cops did they have in this town? Nick thought bleakly. Still, noise was good. If the kindergarten teacher had any brains at all... Let her have one neuron at least.

She did. Shanni knew exactly what she needed to do.

The boy had threatened the stranger—he'd shoot him if they moved—but Shanni couldn't allow herself to worry about that. Her first—her *only* responsibility was to her children. Len and his hostage were no sooner out of the door, concentrating on the advancing police, than she was sending a silent message to Marg with her eyes. Let's get them out of here!

She had to risk talking a little.

'I want absolute silence!' she whispered to the children, forcing herself to stay on the mat so her eyes were level with theirs. Somehow she had to keep calm. 'Not one peep out of anyone. This is a pirate game, just like we've been talking about. So the order is that you stay quiet as mice and stay exactly where you are until I touch you. Then, when I touch you on the shoulder, you run outside to Marg, just as fast as your legs can carry you. But not one sound, or Dirty Dick will win the game.'

Then, with a final commanding glance at the children— daring them to disobey—and one cheeky grin to show them it was still fun—she rose, practically shoved the still boggling Marg toward the back door, and she touched Hugh who'd been standing with Marg. 'Okay, run. Hugh, you first. Now Louise. Go! Now Mary! Sam! Tony! Faster. Good kids. Outside, and Marg will get you right away from Dirty Dick. Go!'

Nick took a deep breath. There were police running toward the place and somehow he had to stop them. Somehow he had to raise his voice.

'Stop! Right now!'

They stopped, but to his horror Nick saw that two of the police had their guns drawn. Great—a gun battle with him as the meat in the sandwich.

He needed to talk and he needed to talk fast! He raised his voice and yelled.

'I'm Nick Daniels, and behind me is Len Harris. Len's jumped bail after armed robbery charges. He has a gun trained on my back and he'll kill me if you come closer.' He was trying to give as much information as he could in the little time he had, but it was as much as he could manage to make his voice work at all. *Let her be moving the kids...*

'I didn't tell you to say who I was.' Len's gun jabbed Nick hard in the back and Nick grimaced with pain. 'Just say... Say, "One step closer I'll kill you."'

There were three policemen now within listening range. They'd been running but had stopped dead at Nick's words.

'One step closer and he'll kill me,' Nick repeated flatly.

'I mean it,' Len yelled, and the gun dug deeper. 'Now... Get back. *Now!*'

Heck, did he have the gun cocked? Somehow Nick had sounded calm enough, but there were rivulets of sweat running down his forehead.

But the police had the message. 'Okay. We're backing up.' The first policeman held out a hand, signalling the others to stop behind him. 'What do you want?'

'I dunno yet,' Len yelled. 'I gotta think. You give me space. I got all these kids in here...'

'Don't touch the children!' The closest policeman's voice rose in fear and Nick looked more closely at the officer. He looked in his thirties—around the right age to have a child of his own in there.

'We're going back inside.' The gun jabbed again into the small of Nick's back. It hurt! 'Don't follow. That's all.'

'I'm telling him to let some of the children go,' Nick

yelled, dragging back against Len's insistent pull. 'He can't keep all of them. Tell him I'm right.' He was desperately buying time here. Len was staring straight out at the policemen, and his attention was solely on the outside. And inside...

Surely there was a back door in the kindergarten? Surely the woman wouldn't be so stupid as to stay still and wait for this crazy kid to return? He had to give her time.

'You can't keep twenty-five kids hostage,' the policeman yelled, confirming Nick's impression. Yep, this officer knew the kindergarten, right down to the number of children inside. He had personal involvement here.

That was good, Nick figured. No policeman was going to try heroics if his kid could be caught in the crossfire.

Were the children moving out? Out of the corner of his eye Nick saw a flutter of movement behind him. A wisp of colour against the building, fast removed. Please...

'I ain't letting any of them go,' Len snarled. 'And you come closer and I kill them. One by one.' He jabbed Nick again, grabbed his collar and hauled him backwards into the kindergarten.

At first sight, Nick thought she'd got them all away. There wasn't a child in sight. But then he saw a neat denimed backside, sticking up from underneath a side table and his heart sank. Surely she hadn't tried to hide?

As Len gave a roar of rage, Shanni turned to face him, her arms cradling a tiny boy.

'You should have gone.'

'Right, and left Harry.' An hour later, they were seated against the wall as far from either door as Len could set them. Len was standing opposite, staring out through a chink in the closed curtains. Every so often he'd swivel to stare at his hostages, and only now had he calmed down enough for them to dare speaking. For a while there Nick had feared for this girl's life.

But she'd stood up to Len as she'd emerged from under the table to face him.

'I don't care who you are or what you're doing, but you don't need twenty-five tiny hostages. You have me, you have this man and you have one child.' She'd tilted her chin, defiant and seemingly fearless. 'And if you hurt Harry—' she'd held the child closer '—then you'll only have one hostage, because you'll have to kill me, too.' And there had been enough steely determination in her voice for Len to know he'd heard the absolute truth.

She'd looked beautiful, Nick thought, stunned. He'd never seen anyone with such courage. This woman took his breath away. And what she'd achieved... Somewhere outside, twenty-four children were being reunited with their parents, with only one remaining here. One emaciated baby with wide eyes and a leg in a cast: a baby who sat ramrod-stiff on Shanni's lap and didn't make a sound.

If only she'd been a little faster... 'Why didn't you get Harry out too?' he asked, looking down at the child. Surely he wasn't old enough for kindergarten.

'You didn't give me enough time,' she whispered. 'He was under the table.'

'Yeah, right.' He didn't understand, but he heard the note of accusation in her voice and it wasn't only about not giving her enough time. Her accusation made him blink.

'You blame me for this?'

'You chased him in here. Of all the stupid...'

'Hey, I didn't!' His voice rose, and he bit his lip and cast a wary glance at Len. Len, though, was too busy looking outside at the gathering forces of the law. 'He saw me at the petrol station and assumed I was after him.'

'You're a cop?'

'A lawyer.'

'Oh, great.' Her voice said what she thought of lawyers in general—and one lawyer in particular.

'This is *not* my fault,' Nick said through gritted teeth— he wasn't used to being talked to like this by a woman.

Shanni glowered darkly and held Harry closer. 'I'm not listening. I need someone to blame, and a city lawyer with a too-thin tie and expensive aftershave will do very nicely, thank you very much.'

He blinked. For heaven's sake... She was...laughing at him?

He must be mistaken. Women didn't laugh at Nick Daniels. And women didn't laugh in situations like this. Her attention was back on the child now, and she was ignoring the reaction she'd had on Nick. Her arms were hugging the little boy, trying to draw his rigid little body into hers.

'Hey, Harry, it's okay. It's okay.' She rocked him back and forth as she'd been rocking him for over half an hour but there was no sound. Was he mute? Nick wondered, watching woman and child. He knew nothing about babies. Maybe all children reacted like this to fear.

'His mum and dad'll be beside themselves with worry,' he ventured.

'No.' Shanni shook her head. 'Harry lives in one of the houses of the local orphanage. His house mum, Wendy, will be waiting outside, though, won't she, Harry?'

Silence. Nothing.

'Is he all right?' Nick stared down at the little boy. There was something wrong here, apart from the cast on his leg. He mightn't know much about children, but he wasn't stupid.

'He's fine.' Shanni sighed. 'As fine as each of us are in this mess.' She bit her lip and then seemed to do an inward shrug. Retrieving a hand from around Harry, she extended it in his direction. 'I'm Shanni McDonald. And this is Harry Lester.'

'I'm Nick Daniels.' He took her hand in his and found it surprisingly warm and strong. Different...

She was a very different woman from the type he was accustomed to, he decided, but he couldn't quite figure out why. Or why she made him feel...odd.

Well, at least she wasn't falling into hysterics on him, he decided thankfully. He managed a faint smile—and found her eyes disconcertingly twinkling at him.

'I could say the same for you,' she said.

'I beg your pardon?'

'I can guess what you're thinking and, like you, I'm really pleased you're not the fainting type. We need a couple of cool heads here.'

A couple of cool heads... Nick blinked. She was implying *she* could help get them out of this mess—and she seemed almost to be able to read his mind!

'Don't do anything,' he said hurriedly. The last thing they needed here was heroics.

'I'm not stupid,' she said with dignity. 'Not like some people I know.' Then she bit her lip and the twinkle appeared again. 'Harry, Mr Daniels might have chased a pirate right into our kindergarten but maybe we should be nice to him. Shall we offer him some milk and fruit?'

'Milk and fruit?'

'It's what you eat,' she said austerely, 'in a kindergarten.' And then, before he could say a word, she raised her voice. 'Len?'

Len wheeled from the window as if she'd yelled, and the gun whirled to point straight at her. To Nick's amazement she didn't react with fear but with purpose, rising to her feet with Harry still cradled in her arms. No fast movements—but determined for all that.

'Sit down!' Len's voice cracked in panic but Shanni simply shook her head.

'I can't,' she said. 'I need to go to the bathroom.'

'No!'

'There are no windows in the bathrooms,' she said evenly. 'Check and see. There's only roof vents, and I'm not that athletic. No one is.' She smiled, and her smile would have stopped a tank in its tracks. 'Len, if you don't let me go, you'll be sorry.'

'I...'

'I bet you want to go, too,' she said thoughtfully. 'What with all this excitement. Tell you what? Why don't you take your gun and Mr Daniels and Harry into the boys' room while I use the girls' room. You can keep your gun on them and I swear I won't go anywhere.'

He stared at her, baffled.

'Make as many threats as you like,' she said calmly. 'You don't need to. I'm promising, and I don't break promises. I will *not* try to escape. You have my word. I won't leave Harry. But if we can't work bathroom arrangements out we're going to be very uncomfortable.'

'Yes...' He thought this through. 'If you try and get away I'll shoot the kid. I mean it.'

'I told you—I won't leave without Harry,' she said, and her eyes were direct and honest—so that even Nick, who didn't trust anyone, trusted her. 'I swear.'

And, to Nick's amazement, Len agreed.

CHAPTER TWO

As HE agreed to almost everything else she suggested through that long afternoon and night. Len might be a criminal with a record a mile long, but he was also still child enough to respond to Shanni's authoritative schoolmarming and cheerful smile. In fact, he almost seemed to like it, and, as night fell and she warmed milk for him, he even gave her a hint of a shy smile in return.

'Ta...'

'Think nothing of it,' she said, ignoring Nick's look of amazement. She glanced at her watch. It was almost ten. After a dinner of bananas, apples and milk there was nothing more she could do to make them comfortable or to defuse the tension. 'I guess we should all try to sleep now.'

That was too much to expect. 'Don't be stupid!' Len clutched his mug of milk in one hand, his gun in the other and stared out into the night like a hunted thing.

There'd be scores of policemen outside now, Nick knew, with sharpshooters, police psychologists—the works. The police had tried over and over to talk to Len through the long afternoon, but his fear hadn't let him take the first step. The phone was off the hook and he was simply ignoring the loud hailer.

It was looking as if it would be a long, long night.

'You don't mind if we try to sleep, then?' Shanni gestured down to the mats they used for the children's naps. She had blankets and pillows piled up—everything they needed.

'Do what you want,' Len almost snarled, and Nick thought, he's tired. He wants to sleep—but he daren't.

So Shanni spread out the bedding, two sets of mats three feet apart. Nick glanced down at them and casually pushed them together.

'It'll be warmer,' he suggested, and Shanni looked thoughtful. But she didn't disagree.

'Come on, Harry,' she said, and slipped down between mat and blankets, holding the child close, as if she really did intend sleeping.

Nick stared down at them for a long moment—and then did the same.

There was nothing else to do but sleep with her!

Weird!

Len had the lights turned off so he could see outside more clearly. Nick lay staring up into the dark. He was trying to sleep on kindergarten mats, for heaven's sake, with a woman and child by his side. He could feel the warmth of Shanni—her arm was brushing his, and he was acutely aware of every movement. Sleeping with a woman had never seemed like this! Strangely, it had never seemed so intimate.

She was some woman! She made him feel...

No! It was hardly the time to think like this now! Think of something else. The child...

Harry hadn't said a word all day, Nick remembered, dragging his thoughts from where they kept straying. Right to the feel of Shanni... The thought of Shanni...

Stop it, Daniels. Get a hold on yourself!

Keep thinking of the child. Harry...

Harry had eaten the fruit Shanni had fed him, and he'd drunk his milk. He'd gone to the bathroom and submitted while Shanni had given him a wash. All the time he'd seemed totally aloof, though his wary eyes had been watching every move anyone made. Now...in the dark, Nick sensed he was still being watched. The little boy was between them, with Shanni's arms around his shoulders, holding tight. Shanni's arms...

'Comfy?' Shanni murmured, and Nick grimaced.

'Comfy as I'll ever be. Would it have hurt to have full-length blankets?' He had blankets draped all over him, but with three-foot kindergarten lengths it took four pieces to cover him.

'We don't get many six-foot students in this place.' Shanni chuckled, and the weird sense of intimacy deepened. But, in the faint light filtering in from outside, Nick saw her cast a glance across at Len. She wasn't focussed entirely on Nick or Harry, then. She was checking their talking wasn't making Len edgy, but Len's attention was all on the outside. It was okay to keep talking. 'Mr Daniels is a bit big for our beds, isn't he, Harry?' she said softly into the dark.

There was no sound from Harry, but he wasn't asleep.

'Does he ever talk?'

'Who, Harry?' Shanni gave Harry a squeeze to which the child didn't respond at all. 'Only when he wants to—which isn't often. Harry's just new at our kinder. He hasn't learned yet that we're his friends and we're never going to hurt him.'

So...the kid lived in an orphanage and he thought adults were things to be feared. Nick frowned, stunned into silence at the unexpected, gut-twisting wrench of sympathy he felt for him.

Which was stupid. This wasn't like him. He didn't get involved emotionally! Ever.

'Come on, Harry, love,' Shanni was whispering. 'Settle down. Let me cuddle you.'

He didn't. His eyes watched everything, supremely distrustful...

'I'll stay awake with Harry,' Shanni suggested. 'You try

and sleep first. Maybe it's not such a good idea for both of us to sleep.'

'I think it's a great idea,' Nick said thoughtfully. They were whispering into the dark and Len seemed to neither know nor care. 'This isn't like the movies. The police know their business, and at least one of the officers out there is personally involved. There's no chance they'll come storming in, guns blazing. Unless Len makes any stupid moves we'll still be here tomorrow, and he's not desperate yet.'

'You know about this? About hostage situations?' For the first time Nick heard a note of fear enter her voice. She wasn't as tough as she sounded, he thought. But, then, neither was he. This wasn't a game.

'I'm a criminal lawyer. I've coped with the aftermath of hostage situations and I know the last thing the police will do is escalate the situation. They'll keep talking. And waiting. They can change shifts and they'll act like they have all the time in the world.'

He smiled across into her worried eyes with what he hoped was his most reassuring smile. He watched her face as she thought this through, and the fear eased a little.

'So tonight Len won't sleep and tomorrow he'll be overtired as well as terrified,' he went on. 'Therefore…we sleep now, so we have our wits about us tomorrow.'

'It sounds sensible,' Shanni whispered into the dark. 'You hear that, Harry?'

'Daddy,' whispered Harry, and Shanni closed her eyes. It hurt.

'Wendy's waiting outside for you, sweetheart.'

'Daddy,' Harry said, and his voice broke with a tiny sob.

'Where's his dad?' Nick asked.

'Dead,' Shanni said shortly. 'Car accident.'

Oh, no…

He didn't get involved. He didn't! But after that one tiny

sob there was nothing else. Harry was holding his grief all to himself.

'Hey...' It was too much for Nick. The child was cradled between them—closer than Nick had ever been to a child before this. He reached over and touched the little boy's face, his arm touching Shanni's as he moved. 'Daddy's not here but I am,' he said, and a part of him couldn't believe what he was saying. 'Will I do—just for now?'

There was a long, long silence. Harry watched him, questioning, and, just as gravely, Nick watched back.

Then, suddenly, as if he could bear it no longer, the massive restraint broke. Harry reached out and put his arms around Nick's neck. He gave a shuddering sob, clung as if he was drowning, and he slumped onto his chest.

He shuddered once more, gave a racking sob that convulsed his whole body, then went absolutely limp.

And then he slept.

What sort of man was this?

Shanni lay awake for far longer than Nick and Harry. The boys slept. The lawyer and the baby.

The contrast was almost ludicrous.

Harry, tiny, fair and frail, with his leg in its fibreglass cast and with the hurts to his small body only just fading.

And Nick Daniels...whoever he was. A city lawyer of some kind. He looked lean and tough and ruthless. Len had run from him because he was afraid, and Shanni didn't blame him. If she'd thought she was in Nick Daniels' power, she'd run too.

He looked like a hawk, she decided. Strong, and not an ounce of spare fat on him. His face was almost chiselled, with a strong jaw line and deep-etched bones. He was so tanned his eyes seemed constantly in shadow, which furthered the impression of an eagle.

And yet... With his tie undone, with the tiny boy's arms

clinging around his neck, he seemed in some strange way almost as vulnerable as the child in his arms.

That was some crazy thought, Shanni figured. Vulnerable? No! This man was a city lawyer with expensive clothes and looks that would make him stand out like a sore toe in Bay Beach.

Thelma, the local laundress, would have kittens if she was asked to clean his suit, Shanni decided. And his ties… The locals had learned long ago that gorgeous fabrics simply disappeared when Thelma got them into her clutches. She loved them and hoarded them as her own. If she ever got her hands on Nick's tie it'd take all his legal wiles to get it back—and Shanni's money was on Thelma.

Good grief! *That* was a crazy thought, she figured, and she almost chuckled into the darkness. Here she was, in a life and death situation, and all she could think of was legal battles between a city lawyer and the Bay Beach laundress!

But it was a good thought, she decided finally. It was a brave thought and it was better than going to sleep thinking of hunger and guns.

She closed her eyes and, to her amazement, she went to sleep with a smile on her face.

When Nick woke, Shanni still slept. He looked across at her in the filtering dawn light and thought how odd that her mouth was curved into a smile in sleep—as if she was having a lovely dream. The little boy was cradled between them and her hand was over him as if she'd protect him even in sleep. Nick's arm was around Harry and she was pressed against it. They were twined together as three.

Like a…family?

The thought was suddenly gut-wrenchingly bitter. How would the likes of Nick know what a family was? This scenario was fantasy-world stuff—not real life.

And real life was intruding. Nick stirred and the fantasy

ended right there. He'd slept with Harry clinging; his neck was screaming its protest and Harry was clinging still. He reached up and tried to loosen the small arms, but Harry muttered in sleep and his hold tightened.

He should pull the child away—but he couldn't make himself do it. Somehow... Instead Nick returned his attention to Shanni, telling himself he needed something to distract him from the discomfort around his neck.

Or maybe...maybe it was that he really wanted to look at Shanni some more. Extend the family fantasy?

She wasn't his type at all, he decided as he watched her. Sure, she was lovely enough, but she was totally unsophisticated in style and much more simply dressed than any woman Nick had ever been attracted to.

She was dressed as a kindergarten teacher, ready for rough-and-tumble with her children. Now her jeans and her too-big-shirt were crumpled from sleep, and her blonde curls were tumbling all over her pillow. There was a smattering of freckles running down her nose, and her lashes were peculiarly dark for one so blonde, but it wasn't mascara that was doing it—they were long and natural and curled upward... Just like her nose. Sort of snub... Pert... Young.

She wasn't his type at all, he decided, and why he should lie here staring at her...

She opened her eyes and she smiled, and his gut kicked in. That smile of hers was a real heart-stopper. Straight from sleep, it lit her face and brightened the room around her as if someone had flicked on a light switch.

'Hi,' she whispered without moving but taking everything in with wide, intelligent eyes. 'Are we still hostages?' Her smile stayed. Where their arms touched was warm—a link of comfort. Or more...

'Yes. We're still hostages.' Good grief, it was all he could do to make his voice work.

'But we're not dead yet.' She yawned and stretched like a cat under her mound of blankets, and the link strengthened as her body stirred against him. 'That's something.'

'Yeah, great.' Try sarcasm, Daniels...

'Well, it is!' Her eyes reproached him. 'Trust a lawyer to look on the gloomy side.'

'There's no need to disparage the legal profession.'

'Oh, I've met some very nice lawyers.' Her eyes twinkled at him, teasing. 'All of them over eighty. It takes them that long to realise they're human after all.'

'Thanks very much.'

'Don't mention it.' The twinkle peeped out again. 'Isn't this cosy?'

'Very cosy.' It was, too—absurdly cosy—but he forced his voice to sound dry. For the life of him he didn't know how else to react. 'My arm's about to drop off.'

'It must be,' she agreed sympathetically. 'But, Nick, it's lovely how he's holding you. Harry hasn't held anyone in the whole time I've known him.'

'I'm honoured.' That was the lawyer in him now, being sardonic, but she ignored it.

'You are indeed,' she said seriously. 'If you knew how hard we've worked to get a link...' And then she paused. 'But...you're not local, are you?'

'No, but...'

'So you're just passing through town.' There was no mistaking her disappointment, and for the life of him Nick couldn't stop a weird warm glow stir through his body—starting from the toes up. And then she killed it. 'We want Harry so much to form a bond with someone.'

She wanted someone for Harry. Of course. What else could she possibly have meant?

'You mean...you'd want me to stay for the kid?'

'Isn't that why women always ask men to stay? Because of the children?' She chuckled. They were still talking in whispers in the near dark and they were almost nose to nose. Over by the window Len either couldn't hear or he didn't care. 'What else did you think I meant?'

What indeed? There was no answer to that one. The glow died—but the link stayed. Her nose was too close!

'So... You're from Melbourne?' He had this almost overwhelming desire to kiss her and she was talking social niceties. It was as much as he could do to figure out what she was talking about.

'I... Yes.'

'And you're in Bay Beach on business?' She sounded politely interested—nothing more.

'I am.' And then he weakened. He might as well tell her. Soon the whole district would know. 'I'm taking over from Judge Andrews. Rotating magistrate.'

'Rotating magistrate!' Her eyes widened, her eyes lit with pleasure and her lovely smile practically enveloped her face. 'Then you're not leaving. You're here for two years. That's fantastic.'

He chewed that over for a bit. 'Why is it fantastic?' he asked cautiously, and here it came. Of course.

'Because Harry likes you.'

'Yes?'

'Yes. He does.' Her eyes darkened and intensified. 'Nick, you mustn't look like that.' She put out a hand and touched the little boy's soft hair. Harry was dead to the world, sleeping the sleep of the exhausted as his body was cradled between them. He'd forced himself to stay awake far too late last night, he hadn't trusted anyone, but in Nick's arms he'd felt safe.

'Harry's had a dreadful time,' she said simply.

'I don't need to—'

'He wasn't wanted,' she went on, ignoring his interruption. 'His mother has two children by a previous marriage and she didn't much like Harry's father. Peter was landed with him at birth.'

'Peter. You mean…the father kept the baby?'

'That's right. It was okay for a while. Peter took Harry with him everywhere, and he loved him to bits. But…almost a year ago he and Harry were in a car accident. Peter was killed. There was a little money from the sale of Peter's house, held in trust for Harry, so Bernadette—Harry's mother—decided she'd take Harry in again. Only…she didn't like or want Harry for himself, and it showed.'

'You mean she mistreated him.'

'Dreadfully.' Her luminous eyes swelled with tears in the dim light. 'He had a smashed leg in the accident and after she took him home she never went near the doctor again. He needed physiotherapy and he never got it. If you knew the condition he was found in when Welfare finally took an interest…' She took a deep breath. 'Anyway, that's in the past. He's safe now, settled in one of the homes of the local orphanage system. And with you he seems to have finally made some contact.'

'I'm not a contactable person,' Nick said bluntly, and Shanni stared from all of six inches away.

'Why ever not?'

'I don't like children.'

'Come on.' She teased him gently with her eyes. 'You've let him give you a numb arm.'

'Only because I didn't want him howling the place down.'

'Liar.'

'It's the truth.'

'Sure.' Her tone said she didn't believe him, but she was moving on. She glanced at her watch and, as she moved, her arm shifted away from his. He was aware of a surge of emptiness as she did. A link broken that he'd valued… But she didn't notice. 'It's six a.m. I wonder how the siege is going?'

'Patiently.'

'They'll wait?'

'For weeks if need be,' Nick told her. 'I know our police force. They'll wait this out.' Please, he added beneath his breath. The thought of anyone bursting in here with guns blazing left him cold.

But... 'A week! We can't live for a week on milk and fruit.' Shanni brushed her curls back from her face and stood up, decision written firmly all over her. 'Good morning, Len,' she said softly, louder than she'd been talking to Nick but still not so loud that she'd wake Harry.

Len wheeled to face them. He looked dreadful, Nick thought dispassionately. The youth looked absurdly young to carry the weapon he had in his hands, and he looked...desperate. The hands that held the gun shook with weariness.

And fear.

Shanni saw.

'You're exhausted,' she said softly. 'You must sleep.'

'I'll sleep when I want to sleep.' Len's voice was an attempt at a vicious growl, but it broke in mid-sentence, marking his youth.

'Okay.' Shanni made a placating gesture and sat down on her mat again. With them sitting Len seemed to relax. As if they couldn't spring on him. But she kept right on speaking. 'Len, I'm really hungry. How about if we order in pancakes?'

'Pancakes!'

'There's a fast-food outlet on the edge of town. They deliver.'

'You've got to be kidding,' Nick said as Len stared in disbelief. 'You're proposing we just ring up and tell them to drive in through the barricades?'

'I don't see why not.' Shanni smiled her very nicest smile at Len—the smile Nick was beginning not to trust. It could make a man do strange things, that smile. 'My brother's a policeman. He's out there somewhere. If I talked to him I reckon we could swing it.'

'No!'

'Pancakes and maple syrup and hot chocolate,' she said beguilingly. 'Steaming hot…'

Len could well have eaten nothing the day before, Nick figured then, watching the look of raw need flash across his face. He must have stolen the car on Thursday night and maybe he'd been on the run ever since. He'd had one glass of milk last night, and all that was left was fruit, cold and unappealing.

'I can do this safely,' Shanni assured him. Then she paused, sneezed, grabbed a tissue from her sleeve and sneezed again. She grinned as she emerged from her tissue. 'Sorry, guys. Hay fever. It's that time of the year. Anyway…' She sneezed again and reassembled. Honestly, she was incorrigible. 'Just let me phone and you can listen to every word I say.'

She gave Len a happy grin, as if he was a friend, and then she sneezed again for good measure. One more sneeze and she was back to entreaty.

'Hey, Len, if you don't like what I do you can shoot me in the toe—and it's not every day I offer a toe. I'm very attached to my toes.'

Len glared.

Shanni sneezed again. She sniffed and recovered and smiled once more. Her very nicest smile…

'Len, I'm just a kindergarten teacher with hay fever,' she said, and the lawyer in Nick made him stare. If he heard this innocent little voice in a witness box he'd know she was lying through her teeth. But Len was no lawyer and she had him dazzled. 'I'm not some hotshot lawyer with brains like my friend, here,' she said, waif-like. 'All I'm saying is that we're hungry and I can organise us a great breakfast. But you'll have to trust me.'

He still glared.

Shanni sneezed. She looked so innocent, Nick thought. She'd pulled off her trainers, she was barefooted, fresh from sleep, and her curls were unbrushed and tangling around her face. She sneezed again and he wondered how on earth she'd ever got this job. In charge of a kindergarten? She didn't look as if she should be in charge of anything. But...there was this tiny twinkle behind her eyes that he mistrusted...

'Sorry. Drat my stupid hay fever,' she said weakly. 'Late spring's my worst season. They're cutting hay all around the town and mornings are dreadful. And I'm so hungry. Len, please let me ring my brother. You can listen to every word.'

The room held its breath.

And finally Len nodded. Between pancakes, sneezes and smiles he seemed bewitched. As Nick was.

'Okay. Be fast. And I'm listening.'

Shanni smiled. She sneezed once more and crossed to the phone.

And the twinkle stayed.

'Hello?' She dialled emergency and to her relief it took her straight through to the command post outside. They must have had the line rigged so every call was monitored.

'Police here.'

'It's Shanni McDonald,' she said.

'Shanni...' She recognised the voice of the local police inspector, and it was hoarse with worry. A siege like this must be every policeman's nightmare. 'Are you okay, lass?'

'We're fine.' Len nudged her in the ribs with the gun. On the mat Harry stirred in Nick's arms and Nick sat up, cradling the child against him. They looked sort of cute, Shanni thought, looking across at the out-of-town magistrate and his baby—before concentrating carefully on sneezing again. Some things were important. Apart from cute lawyers...

And Len's patience was running out. The gun dug into her ribs, harder this time, and she turned her attention back to what she was doing.

'Inspector, we're very hungry,' she said. 'All of us.'

'I can understand that.'

'You're not planning on starving us out?'

'Tell us what you want.'

She took a deep breath. 'Pancakes,' she said. 'Hot food and plenty of it. We thought fast-food pancakes, maple syrup, and hot chocolate. From Don's Diner.'

'We can do that. How will we get it in?'

'Have someone put it on the doorstep. Len won't shoot anyone carrying pancakes, will you, Len?' The youth was listening to every word being said, standing right against her as she talked while the gun stayed pressed into her side. She sneezed and he backed off a bit.

'Inspector...?'

'Yes.'

'I need my hay fever pills,' she added. 'Rob will know. The strong night ones.'

'I didn't say anything about no...' Len started, but Shanni sneezed again. She gave him an apologetic smile.

'Please?' she said nicely, and he grimaced.

'Okay,' he snapped. 'And tell him I want a helicopter.'

'That might be harder than pancakes and hay fever pills,' Shanni said mildly, and Len swore and grabbed the phone.

'I want a helicopter,' he told the policeman. 'To get me away from here.'

'You'll leave the hostages behind?' The inspector's voice was carrying and Shanni could hear every word.

'They'll come with me. I'll dump them where I'm going.'

'It'll take time to organise,' the policeman said urgently.
'Maybe all day. There's been a storm north of here and
emergency services are stretched.'

'A helicopter by tonight or someone gets it.'

'I'll try.'

'And get them pancakes.' Len crashed the phone back
on the cradle and went back to staring out the window.
While Nick watched Shanni. Who'd forgotten to sneeze…

'Are we having pancakes?' Harry asked, rubbing his
sleepy eyes, and Nick nodded and gave him an impulsive
hug. When really he wanted to hug Shanni.

'Thanks to your clever kindergarten teacher we might
well be having pancakes.' Then, as Shanni sat down beside
them again, Nick lowered his voice so only she could hear
and said, 'And hay fever tablets to boot. How about that?
If you're thinking what I'm thinking, Shanni McDonald,
that could make us all feel very much better!'

The pancakes arrived and were delicious, though for the
life of him Nick couldn't urge Harry from his knee. Shanni
fed him his pancakes in pieces like a little bird, and every
time Nick tried to put him aside the child forgot about food
and turned and clung.

Nick found it claustrophobic—and Shanni's delighted
smile made it worse.

'I don't like children,' Nick said through gritted teeth,
and she chuckled.

'Yeah, right. I can see that. But you don't have to like
children. Just Harry.'

And Len? Len ate his pancakes as if he hadn't seen food
for a week. Shanni had opened the door and pulled the tray
inside and Len had fallen on it as if all his Christmases had
come at once. Luckily whoever had organised it had decided to provide enough to feed the teeming masses; otherwise there'd have been none for anyone else.

'That was wonderful,' Shanni said after her third pancake. She sneezed as she carried the litter back to the bench and fetched the mugs of hot chocolate. 'And what's coming is better still.' She twisted the cap off the bottle of hay fever pills. 'My pills! Sorry guys. Now I can stop sneezing.'

She carried mugs of hot chocolate over to Nick and Harry, and then to Len at his watching post by the window.

'Thank you for letting us eat,' she said softly, smiling down at him. 'It was kind.'

'Yeah...all right.' He looked longingly at the chocolate. It was thick and creamy with a melting marshmallow floating on top, but the sight disturbed him. 'We shoulda got coffee. Coffee'd keep us awake.'

'I'm sorry.' She sounded so contrite it was pathetic. 'If you don't want this, I'm sure Harry would like two mugs.'

'I'll drink it,' he snapped. 'Go away.'

'Hot chocolate.' Nick looked thoughtful as he sipped. 'Now, why didn't you order coffee, Shanni McDonald?'

'We have coffee here for Marg and I to use.'

'Instant.' His tone said what he thought of that.

'This isn't metropolitan Melbourne,' she snapped. 'You've come a long way from cappuccino society here.'

'I understand that.' He grimaced. He certainly had. 'But I'd assume your fast-food chain provides decent coffee. Not as sweet, of course. Or maybe...' He cast a glance at Len, who'd drained his chocolate and was back staring intently out of the window. 'Maybe not as disguising?'

'Just drink your chocolate and shut up,' Shanni snapped.

'And wait and see?'

'And wait and see.'

'Your sneeze seems to have stopped. Those pills must be very effective.'

'I do hope so,' she said simply—and waited.

*   *   *

They waited an hour.

Len was rocking on his stool by the window. The curtains were still drawn and Shanni hadn't turned on the light.

'It's cosier in the almost dark,' she said, and lay on her back and told Harry the story of *The Very Hungry Caterpillar*.

Still within the safety of Nick's arms, Harry listened and Shanni thought it was the first time she'd ever known Harry to listen at all.

She held her breath and waited.

And it wasn't just the pills she was waiting on...

It was strange, Nick decided. Surrealistic. For Nick, accustomed to living life at full speed, to be forced to lie and hold a child and listen to the exploits of a make-believe caterpillar... He'd never done such a thing in his life.

The whole world held its breath.

Over at the window, Shanni could sense Len was listening too. And waiting. She made her voice calm and warm and even and when Harry dropped off to sleep again she wasn't surprised.

What did surprise her was Nick. Gently he disengaged Harry's clutching fingers, let the little one slip sideways onto the pillows and then, with a questioning look at Shanni—a 'help-me-with-this' look—he rose and crossed steadily to Len at the window. Shanni watched him every step of the way, her hand coming down to cradle Harry so he wouldn't notice Nick's absence.

'Len?' Nick said softly.

His head jerked up. He was so close to sleep... 'Yes?'

'You're cold, boy.' He pushed the reading chair forward—the only comfortable chair in the kindergarten. It was padded, with a high back, and he tossed a couple of cushions on for good measure. 'It might take hours for the helicopter to arrive. If you're not comfortable your muscles might cramp up and you'll fall off your stool. Use this one.' He pushed the chair against the window. Then, as Len hesitated, he threw a couple of blankets on top.

'Make yourself comfortable,' he suggested.

'Why are you doing this?' Len's face was all suspicion.

'If you fall off the stool, chances are that gun will go off,' Nick said bluntly. 'Then you'll have every cop in the country storming in. Neither of us wants that.' And then he grinned. 'And you let us have pancakes.'

His smile was beguiling—even Shanni was beguiled, for heaven's sake, and this man was a lawyer!—and it worked a treat. Len didn't answer—he glared—but he grudgingly moved from his hard stool to the comfortable chair. And when Nick offered blankets, he threw them over his knees and almost managed a smile of thanks.

'It'll get better,' Nick said, and Shanni practically gaped in astonishment at the sympathy in his voice. 'This isn't the end of the world, you know.'

'What would you know about it?' Defiance—but also fear.

'I know you haven't killed anyone. I know you're young and young offenders don't go to jail. They go to remand homes where, if they want, they can learn a trade. I know there's a heart under that tough exterior...'

'I can't...'

'And you love cars,' Nick said softly. 'I can see that.' He motioned out of the window to where the smashed grey Mercedes lay between them and the police. 'If you have to steal cars, at least you steal cars with class. It's taken a darn sight more skill to steal this baby than a cheaper job.'

His dark eyes twinkled down at Len and it wasn't just Len who was mesmerised. Shanni was speechless. This was a whole new facet to the man. Up until now she hadn't been able to see past the smooth exterior, but now...there was a human being in there somewhere. 'If you're willing to learn about mechanics while you're in remand school, I'd bet there'd be luxury car dealers who'd be prepared to take you on,' he said.

'Yeah? Like who?'

'Like my uncle,' Shanni interjected, smiling up at Nick as if he was talking absolute sense. 'He runs a dealership. I know one of his lads has a police record, but my uncle doesn't care—as long as he keeps straight now and knows how to fix his engines.'

'He wouldn't employ me.'

'You'd have to do your time first,' Shanni said thoughtfully. 'But if you put your time in the remand home to good use...'

'I ain't going to remand school.'

'Hey, Len, just think about it,' Nick urged gently. 'While we sleep.'

'Another story, I think,' Nick said as he returned to his mat. Shanni's eyes were wide with appreciation.

As were Nick's. This woman was extraordinary. As he'd made Len warm and comfortable and soothed his terror, she'd given Len what he most needed—hope. Len was dead tired, and, if Nick's guess was right, he was full of sleeping pills. Now all they had to do was set the mood—and Shanni was right onto that.

'How about if I read *Goodnight, Goodnight*?' she suggested.

'Harry's asleep already,' Nick said reluctantly. He'd lifted Harry into his arms again, unthinking, as if it was an instinctive movement. It was starting to feel as if the child belonged there.

'He might wake up if I don't keep reading,' Shanni said softly. 'If I keep my reading going I'll soothe him into sleeping for ever.'

Or who else might she soothe into sleep?

It was so...seductive.

Shanni had turned on the heater and the room was warm—almost over-warm. The huge breakfast had made Nick feel so sated he almost needed sleep again himself, even though it was only two hours since he'd woken. The child in his arms slept on and on, catching up on missed time.

Shanni's voice was low and sweet and melodic—soothing him toward rest.

If Nick hadn't been watching Len...

But he was. He was watching Len like a hawk. The gun was slowly slipping. It must be *so* heavy.

Please let those outside not use the loud hailer or try to contact him again, Nick thought, but if Shanni's brother had twigged as to why she wanted the hay fever tablets then they wouldn't be so stupid.

They weren't.

Shanni read and Nick watched Len—and Nick watched Shanni. He watched the gentle rise and fall of her breast, and he listened to the soft lilting of her voice. If I was three years old this is where I'd like to go to kindergarten, he thought dazedly, and had to shake himself. No one had ever read him stories. Not ever!

For heaven's sake, he was thirty-two years old. This was stupid. He was feeling like this just because it was a novelty. A situation like this...

A woman like Shanni...

He'd never met anyone like her.

And finally her voice fell away to nothing.

And she'd succeeded.

'He's asleep,' she said softly. At the window, Len's face had fallen forward so his chin was resting on his chest. His gun had fallen to one side in the chair and his hands were lifeless. His chest rose and fell in a slow, steady rhythm.

'Len?' Shanni asked softly.

'Leave him be for a bit,' Nick said. 'We've worked on this. Let's not spoil it by hurrying.'

'*We've* worked on this?'

He grinned at that, tension easing. 'Okay, smartyboots. *You've* worked on it. How many tablets did you give him?'

'Four at twenty-five milligrams.'

'Enough to stop the worst sneezing.'

'Even mine,' she said virtuously. She wrinkled her nose and her eyes danced. 'See? Not even a sniffle.'

'Miraculous. How many did you take?'

'Hmm. Somewhere between zero and none. I can't quite remember.'

He smiled and they waited on, both knowing that once Len was deeply asleep they had nothing to fear. Ten minutes. Fifteen. It was strangely intimate: sitting in a pile of bedding holding the child in his arms with Shanni watching over them.

'He has such huge problems,' she said out of the blue.

'Who?' Were they talking about Len?

They weren't. 'Harry, of course.' She sighed, placing a hand on Harry's mop of fair curls. 'I'm so worried about him. They're threatening to put him into a home for psychologically disturbed children.'

'Is he?'

'Psychologically disturbed?' She shrugged. 'Maybe. Wouldn't you be if your dad was dead and your mother and stepfather hated you?' And then she frowned at the look on Nick's face. 'Why? What have I said?'

'Nothing.' He somehow put aside shadows of past hurt and shook his head. 'This has nothing to do with me. Or you, either, as far as I can see. He's just one of your students, isn't he? What do you get from taking the worries of the world onto your shoulders?'

'Meaning you think I'm stupid for trying?'

'Maybe.' He shrugged.

She gave him a long, measuring look. 'No. You don't

mean that. For a lawyer, I thought you were pretty good to Len just then.'

'I'm a magistrate. I have to learn niceties.'

'Legal niceties. Not human niceties. But...you were nice just now. It wasn't all an act.'

How did she know that? She didn't!

'So how about you, then?' he demanded, changing tack. Talking about him made him feel like running a mile. 'Surely your family—your uncle with the car dealership— wouldn't seriously think about employing such a kid?'

'There's no hope for him if someone doesn't,' she said sadly. 'So maybe it's just as well there are people like my family in the world. People who care.'

'People who'll get walked all over.'

'Says you.' She shrugged. 'The nice magistrate who tries so hard not to be. Nice, I mean.' And then she smiled, letting him off the hook where he was beginning to squirm. 'Anyway, maybe...' She cast a long look across at Len— and another at Harry. 'While we have both our children sound asleep, I think it's time we got ourselves out of here, don't you?'

'I couldn't agree more. I'll get the gun.'

It was time to leave. But there was a part of him—a part which he didn't understand in the least—that didn't want to leave at all.

There was no choice. Move...

But when he went to hand over Harry, the child's arms tightened like a vice, and if Nick had tried to disengage him he would have woken and sobbed.

So when the kindergarten door opened and Shanni, Nick and Harry emerged, to the huge relief of the waiting constabulary, it was the new town magistrate who was holding the baby, and it was the kindergarten teacher who was holding the gun.

CHAPTER THREE

AND after that it was over—sort of. Police officers surged into the building and emerged with one dazed sixteen-year-old who looked half asleep and as if he didn't know what was happening.

'Please look after him,' Shanni said softly as he emerged, handcuffed and secured. 'He's just a scared kid.'

But the police were taking no chances. He was taken away, sirens screaming, while Nick and Shanni blinked in the unaccustomed daylight and Harry stirred in Nick's arms and started to sob.

A woman—in her late twenties, dishevelled and fearful—emerged from the crowd and tried to take him from Nick's arms. 'Harry. Oh, baby, we've been so worried. Come to Wendy.'

This, then, must be the woman in charge of Harry's home within the orphanage, but Harry was unimpressed. He clung desperately to Nick, and as she tried to take him he screamed.

But Nick had had enough. There was nothing more he could do. He unfastened the desperate fingers and placed the weeping bundle of baby into the woman's outstretched arms.

'He's all yours.'

'No! I want to stay. I want to stay with my Nick.' Harry was screaming with desperation, and Shanni reached forward to hug him.

'Harry, don't worry. Nick's staying here for two years. Maybe we can visit...'

46

He had no intention of travelling down that road. No way!

'We can visit you, Nick?' Shanni asked, and something snapped.

'I don't think so.'

'Why ever not?' She sounded astounded.

This was blackmail, he thought desperately. He had to get out of here—fast! And it was kinder to be blunt.

'See that mountain up there?' He'd had more than he needed of this emotional heart-pull. What a way to start a new life! 'Harry, look at the mountain,' he told him. He raised his voice. 'Now!'

He could still get through to him. Harry stopped sobbing for long enough to stare up to where Mount Borrowah towered over the town.

'That's where I live,' Nick said flatly—definitely. 'I'm sorry, mate, but visiting me's impossible.' He softened then, just a little. 'But it was great to meet you. You be good for Wendy, now.'

And he turned away before he could see the child's face crumple into despair.

Then followed the police debriefing. Hours of it, with question after question. What had happened? What threats had been made? Nick and Shanni were interviewed together and separately, and by the time they were finished Nick conceded that the local police force knew their stuff. They'd get a solid conviction.

It was a major crime, he thought ruefully. Damn. There'd now been one major crime in Bay Beach but he couldn't be involved as magistrate because he was a witness. The committal proceedings would be heard somewhere else.

Which left him still with fishing licences and farm disputes to look forward to. Terrific!

Finally, with interviews complete and after knocking back offers of counselling and psychological help, he

emerged to find the police inspector waiting to greet him
in his new capacity as magistrate.

'Mr Daniels.' His hand was gripped in a massive paw.
'Welcome to Bay Beach. I'm sorry your arrival turned into
such a mess. This place isn't always so exciting.'

Great. He made himself say something polite and non-
committal while behind him, Shanni emerged from her own
interview room. There were a dozen or so people waiting.
They'd been silent as Nick had talked to the inspector but
now they surged forward, engulfing Shanni in a sea of hugs
and laughter and relief. When they finally released her,
Nick was introduced to what must have been almost the
entire population of the town.

Shanni looked exhausted. Since Nick's mention of the
mountain to Harry, she'd been decidedly cool, but she was
still in control enough to stay polite.

'Nick, these are my parents. This is my brother, Rob—
he's a senior constable here. Mary's my sister and she's
your clerk of courts. Here's Sam, Hatty, Will and Louise—
they're all my younger brothers and sisters. Grandma,
Grandpa, Aunt Merle…Uncle Simon—he's the one with
the car yard. Uncle Simon, I want you to write a letter for
me. Everybody, this is Nick Daniels, the town's new magistrate. He lives up on Borrowah Mountain. I don't think!'

They didn't understand that, but Nick was surged on,
regardless, and his hand was wrung until it felt as if it
would drop off.

'We're so grateful you were here to take care of our
Shanni,' Shanni's grandmother quavered and, to Nick's
astonishment, Shanni's brothers and sisters hooted with
laughter. He must have looked stunned, because Guy
McDonald, Shanni's father, noticed.

'Don't look like that, Nick.' The elderly farmer clapped
Nick on the shoulder. 'I'm sure you did well, boy, but we
know Shanni isn't a shrinking violet. All last night, when

the rest of the town were worrying themselves sick about their kindergarten teacher, Shanni's mother and I were wondering whether the kid would get out of there alive.'

'I was never going to shoot him,' Shanni said, affronted.

'No, dear, but you could have talked him into shooting himself,' her mother said comfortably. 'And when Rob rang and asked what Louise took for night-time hay fever...'

'You mean...you don't get hay fever?' Nick demanded, staggered.

'Louise does,' Shanni said blithely. 'Didn't I sneeze well? When Louise has hay fever she blows us away, and the medicine she takes at night knocks her out so hard she snores the roof off.'

'I do not!' Louise glared.

'Do, too.' There was general laughter, and then the police station door burst open. A large young man came striding in, looking deeply anxious. He seemed every inch a farmer—open, weathered face with eyes creased by the sun, moleskins, flannelette shirt, wide-brimmed hat... It only needed a straw sticking out of the side of his mouth to complete the picture.

The man was in no mood for interruptions—or introductions. He was looking for his woman.

'Shanni!' He walked straight to Shanni, gathered her into his arms and he held her as if there was no tomorrow. And she submitted to his embrace as if she belonged there.

Which made Nick feel...weird? But there was nothing he could do but watch and listen.

'Shanni, love,' the stranger was saying, 'I took cattle over to the sales at Warrbook and I've only just got back to hear this. Hell! Love, are you okay? I'll kill the...'

'Hush.' She was being raised right off her feet as she was hugged. As she smiled down into the stranger's eyes,

Nick was aware of a sharp stab of something that might have been jealousy.

No. Ridiculous thought. There was nothing to be jealous of here, for heaven's sake.

'I'm fine,' Shanni was saying, struggling to find her feet. She motioned to Nick. 'Nick, this is John Blainey. John, Nick's our new magistrate. He was taken hostage, too.'

'And you looked after my girl.' Nick's hand was seized and wrung again until his wrist felt broken. 'You got her out of there. I owe you...'

'I think you'll find Shanni got herself out of there,' Nick said wryly. 'I just babysat.'

The man stared—and then he grinned. 'You can still joke. That's fantastic.' He turned and held Shanni tight again. 'That does it, sweetheart. We'll get married. I know I don't have the house built yet, but if you think I'm going to let you run yourself into danger again...'

'By teaching kindergarten?'

'By doing anything without me,' John said stolidly. 'I know how to protect my own, and I'll protect you.'

He needed to get out of here, Nick decided. As, obviously, did the rest of Shanni's family. They were all watching the happy couple with expressions ranging from resigned to nauseous.

'I'm off to collect my car,' Nick said, and Rob stepped forward with an expression that said he'd be glad to help—in fact he'd be glad to get out of there as fast as Nick wanted.

'I'll give you a lift.'

But Shanni was breaking away, turning within John's hold.

'Nick, thank you.'

'For running you into danger? For scaring Len into the kindergarten?'

'Oh, I've forgiven you for that,' she said blithely, and

grinned at his pained expression. 'I know it wasn't your fault. I said it because I like to see lawyers wriggle, so I'm not even going to sue. But thank you anyway.'

'It's me who should be thanking you.'

'Yep,' she said happily and grinned. 'And Louise. It was her tablets did the trick. But for Harry...'

'I didn't do anything.'

'You did,' she said urgently. 'He hugged you. And you still can do something. You still can help. I know you said that stupid thing about the mountain but you were stressed. If we can keep that connection up...'

'I'm not prepared to do that,' he said flatly, and she stared.

'Why ever not?'

'I told you. I don't like kids.'

'You don't like Harry?'

'Shanni, I have a new job here that's going to take all my time,' he said desperately, and she smiled.

'Right. Magistrate at Bay Beach. Full-time job.'

'Don't badger the man, Shanni,' her mother said mildly. 'He's only just walked into the town. Give him at least a few days before you start involving him in any of your save the world missions.'

Shanni wrinkled her pert nose and her eyes twinkled. 'A few days?'

'At least,' her mother said.

Silence.

Then... 'Okay, Nick Daniels,' she said at last. 'You have a few days' grace and then we'll see what we can do to puncture that cool, calm exterior. Oh, and Nick...?'

'Yes?'

'Grandma here's a great seamstress.'

'Pardon?' He was totally at sea.

'You'll want to get those ties widened.' Her smile was gently teasing. 'Magistrates in this town command a bit of

respect; they wear ties, and that's not a tie. That's a shoelace. Grandma, do you call that a tie?'

Her grandmother obediently inspected the slip of expensive Italian silk which was now tugged loose around Nick's
open collar. 'Hmm,' she said, disapproving, and Shanni
nodded.

'*Hmm* is right, Grandma. It'll have to be widened. Nick's
yet to learn that the only impression designer labels give
around here is that he doesn't belong.'

Shanni followed her mother's orders. Nick didn't see her
for five days.

In those days life settled into the pattern he'd expected—
and more so. He was given an apartment above the courthouse, which suited him fine—no garden to look after and
the windows looked out over the sea almost all the way to
Tasmania. He even had a balcony he could use to appre-
ciate the view—which he didn't. He kept the door closed.

The courthouse was old and majestic and sleepy, as was
everything about this town. Mary, Shanni's eldest sister,
was his clerk of courts. Comfortably married to the local
newsagent, with two little boys at school, she knew everything and everybody in Bay Beach, and Nick found himself
thinking it would be easier for everyone concerned if Mary
took over the running of the whole courthouse. She practically did anyway.

'This is Red Barring. Red's up for abalone fishing without a licence,' she told him on his second case. 'He'll plead
that he only caught them for a family celebration, but he
used that excuse the last time and the time before. Everyone
knows he sells them on the black market.'

'You're not supposed to tell me this,' Nick said faintly,
and Mary grinned.

'So you didn't hear me saying it. But it'd be a pity if
you were taken in by Red's baby-blue eyes. He's a thief

and a bully, and he's poaching abalone that fishermen have paid big money for the licences to fish. And when Sam Netherfield's boat ran aground last month and he realised his insurance had lapsed, Red didn't put in a cent to the appeal. Not one cent! Even though Sam was a character witness for Red at his last trial.'

It was all totally improper—but when Red stood before the bench and faltered in a whiny voice that he'd just caught the few abalone for his wife's birthday and a tough fine would send him to the wall, it was sort of hard—if not impossible—for Nick to refrain from giving the police authority to look at the man's finances and report back to the court in a week.

And, at the ludicrous look of dismay on the man's face, he knew it would be stupid to ignore Mary entirely.

But her interference went beyond work.

'What are you interested in?' she demanded on his third day at work.

'Interested in?'

'Mmm.' She beamed. 'What are your hobbies? You must have some. All work and no play doesn't make for a nice, well-balanced magistrate.'

'Did you know you're as bossy and interfering as your sister?'

'I try,' she said smugly. 'Actually I'm older than Shanni so I think I'm better at it. I've had more practice. Now, I'm in the local repertory and we need new members. Can you sing?'

'No!'

It didn't faze her. 'No matter. There's spots as extras. Or we need painters backstage.'

'No!'

'Okay.' She took the rebuff unabashed. 'There's a sailing school on Saturdays, there's chess clubs, there's canoeing, there's angling, there's...'

'Mary, I am not interested in joining clubs.'

'Why ever not?' She was astonished.

'I have plenty to do to keep me employed.'

'Like what?' She fixed him with a look that was re-
markably like her sister's. It was totally disconcerting.
'Your work here is hardly *Go, Go, Go*. What else do you
intend to do in this town?'

What else indeed? Nick took the case file he'd come out
to retrieve, retreated to his office and glowered.

What?

In the city his work had been eighty hours a week plus.
That was the way he liked it. He thrived on work. And his
spare time? He filled it with restaurants, plays, films and
art shows, all with different women...

There was a dearth of restaurants, plays, films and art
shows around here, he thought desperately. *And* beautiful
women.

'Nick...' There was yet another knock on the door and
he sighed.

'I'm busy,' he called.

'Nonsense.' The door opened and Mary walked right in.
Followed by Shanni...and followed by Harry, and his heart
kicked at the sight of the pair of them.

Shanni was just as he remembered though not as dishevelled as after a night of being held hostage. She was now
wearing a soft pink print dress which was bare around her
shoulders and suited her perfectly. Her curls were tied back
with a pale pink and blue ribbon. She looked happy, young
and carefree, and her smile enfolded everyone in the room.
It was Mary's smile and then some. A knockout smile!

'Hi,' she said. 'Mary said you weren't busy.'

'Mary said...' Something would have to be done about
Mary. Soon!

'She also said your lunch-hour is between one and two,

but today you have no more court cases until three. So Harry and I came to take you out to lunch.'

By her side, Harry said absolutely nothing. He was dressed in simple shorts and T-shirt as he'd been wearing the last time Nick saw him, and the cast on his leg looked absurdly heavy for such a little one. And he was silent. Waiting.

For what? Nick knew. Harry held onto Shanni's hand and he looked at Nick with eyes that said he was waiting to be struck. Or…he was waiting for Nick to say no.

Same thing.

'I don't think I can…' Nick tried to prevaricate but it sounded weak, even to him. For heaven's sake, he did *not* want to get involved here. But he didn't want to hurt the child…

'We aren't looking for anything formal, are we, Harry?' Shanni told him, choosing to ignore his hesitation. 'But Thursday is my half-day off, Harry wanted to see you and Mary tells us that you're free.'

'I'm busy,'

'Don't be silly. There's nothing I can't handle here,' Mary said blithely, beaming at her sister in friendly conspiracy. 'Off you go and enjoy yourself. It'll do you good to get out into the fresh air.'

'I don't need fresh air.'

'Oh, for heaven's sake.' Mary assumed her severest look, facing him with an expression that said, No nonsense or you'll stay in after school and do two hundred lines. She used Shanni's school-marm tone. 'You sound like this town will bite, Nick Daniels. There's nothing out there to be afraid of, and Shanni will take good care of you.'

Then Mary and Shanni both beamed.

What was a man to do? 'I'm being railroaded,' he said weakly.

'Of course,' Mary agreed. 'It's what the McDonald girls

are good at. We've been trained from birth by a very railroading mama. And grandma. And great-grandma come to that. Shanni, make him take his tie off.'

'Take your tie off,' Shanni said. 'You can't eat fish and chips on the beach when you're wearing a designer shoelace.'

'I'm not…' He rose and backed off.

'Yes, you are,' Mary said, and she put her hands behind him and shoved him toward the door. 'Know when you're beaten, Your Worship. Out you go and don't come back before three. That's an order.'

He stood on the pavement and couldn't think of a single thing to say. Shanni was grinning like a Cheshire cat and, beside her, Harry was simply looking. And looking and looking, as if he couldn't get enough of him.

'Shanni…' He was starting to sound inane. He was starting to *feel* inane!

'I've ordered fish and chips,' she said, ignoring him. 'We're collecting them down at the wharf in five minutes.'

'What if I don't want to come?' He sounded pathetic!

'Of course you want to come,' she said kindly. 'You just don't think you do. Harry and I are here to change your mind. Shall we take your car—or walk?'

'I don't…'

'Don't want to drive? Okay.' She beamed. 'It's not far. Harry doesn't like cars and he's been practising with the new heel on his cast like anything. And please, take your tie off.'

'No.'

'You look silly with it on.' She twinkled up at him in the sunlight. 'But it's the same one you were wearing when we first saw you. Don't you have a change of clothes?'

'I just brought the one suit. I'm heading back to Melbourne at the weekend.' He'd go nuts if he couldn't.

'Now that's a waste of a weekend if ever I heard one,' she said. 'Spending it in the city changing designer ties!'

And she smiled straight at him—and, despite himself, he was forced to smile right back. Unbelievable! And then he found himself walking at her side down toward the harbour. Harry clumped on bravely on her other side, clutching her hand and occasionally venturing a peep at him around the soft folds of her dress.

'Do you never go to Melbourne?' Nick asked, trying to think of something to say to stop him sounding even more pathetic. As a lawyer and magistrate he was used to facing the world on his terms. It wasn't often the world had him as off balance as this.

'I did my training there,' she told him. 'But I hated it. I came back here every weekend to get my fix of sea air and laid-back country lifestyle.'

'So you admit you need your fix of sea air. Well, I need my fix of city. We're equally addicted, Miss McDonald.'

'We are indeed,' she agreed equably. 'Equally nuts, but if we're comparing the sea to the city I know which I'd rather. What do you think, Harry?' She tugged the little boy forward, scooped him up and placed him so he was between the two of them. 'Do you think we're nuts?'

Harry considered. 'No,' he said at last, seriously, and Shanni chuckled her delight. She really did have the loveliest chuckle.

'You're wonderful, Harry,' she told him. Then she looked down at him. He was walking bravely but the cast must be a pain. 'Do you want Nick to carry you?'

'No.'

That was definite enough, Shanni considered. 'Okay. What about playing One, Two, Three, Jump?'

Harry didn't know what she meant. His small face stared up at his kindergarten teacher in mute enquiry.

'We need to teach him,' she told Nick, but Nick shook his head, as in the dark as Harry.

'Sorry.'

'Sorry, what?' She stared at him.

'I don't know what you're talking about.'

That stopped her dead. She whirled to face them, staring from Nick down to Harry and back to Nick again. 'You mean…you *both* don't know One, Two, Three, Jump?'

'Enlighten our ignorance,' Nick said dryly, knowing she was about to do just that.

But she gave him a strange look—reassessing. It was an odd sideways look, and it left Nick feeling disturbed. As if she was probing where he didn't want to be probed.

'It's very simple,' she said at last, falling in again beside them, but still with that disturbed look on her face. They'd left the single line of shops in the main street behind and were walking down the hill to where the boats were tied up in the harbour below. 'One, Two, Three, Jump requires two adults and one child. We have all the prerequisites right here. Nick, take Harry's hand.'

'But…'

'You quibble, we can't play,' she said direfully. 'No quibbling. Take Harry's hand.'

There was nothing for it. Nick put his hand down and took Harry's fingers in his. Harry looked high up into his face, and then stared intently at their linking—his tiny hand in Nick's large one. Then, very slowly, Harry smiled. He turned and headed on down the hill between his two anchors, stumping gamely on his cast, heading into the wind. As if he'd just had a win of gargantuan proportions.

'Now we're ready,' Shanni announced, and if Nick thought he saw a glimmer of a tear on her eyelashes then surely he was imagining it. She swung Harry's arm. 'One…two…three…!' And before he realised what he was doing, Nick was swinging Harry's little body out before him.

'Jump!'

The tiny boy flew high, held safely between them and, when Harry landed, the look on his face of absolute incredulity that anything like this could be happening to him made Nick falter.

Damn, he might be sure there were tears on Shanni's eyelashes, but what the heck was the lump doing in *his* throat?

There was nothing for it now but to do it all over again. They One, Two, Three, Jumped all the way to the fish shop, and then Nick held the fish-and-chip parcel in one hand and Shanni carried the drinks in another so they could keep on One, Two, Three, Jumping all the way to the beach.

And finally Nick found himself sitting on the sand by the sea, fish and chips spread out before him, and he had absolutely no idea in the world how he'd come to be there.

CHAPTER FOUR

To HIS surprise, they ate in silence.

Nick was no longer sure what he expected of this girl, but silence surely wasn't it. She'd chatted and laughed all the way to the beach, but now, sitting on the sand with Harry on her knee and a spread of fish and chips beside her, she had subsided into a silence that Nick found almost disconcerting.

Not that he didn't welcome it. He needed time to get his breath back.

So he ate the fillets of fish that must surely have only been caught that morning, and he crunched on the golden chips and he absorbed the silence. It was peaceful. It was right, but it was...strange.

As were the sensations. The sand was sun-warmed and soft, and the wind was blowing gently in across the rolling waves. The beach was pristine. There were no footsteps for miles—no one had been on this beach since high tide. The town was clustered round a horseshoe bay—the Bay Beach the town was named after—but Shanni had led them down the track to the back beach, which was the beach the tourists didn't use. Miles wide, with golden sand stretching away into the distance, there were ancient Norfolk pines at its higher reaches casting sentinels of shade across the sand-hills. There was nothing else.

They might as well be the first man and first woman and first child ever to sit on this beach, and, with the silence, it was weird.

When had he last sat on a deserted beach like this?

Never, he thought, and the knowledge was suddenly

bleak. He was a child of the city, who'd never had parents to take him anywhere.

He was like Harry.

No!

He wasn't going to think like that, he decided harshly, because that was the way of attachment. That was what this girl wanted, he knew. This outing was planned with one thing in mind—to establish a link between Nick and the little boy she was holding.

'Finished your chips?' She was smiling at him, still with that strange look in her eyes that said she was searching for something deeper than an answer about the chips. What was she seeing? He didn't want to know.

'Yes. Thank you.' They'd bought far too many.

Shall I feed them to the seagulls?' Harry asked, and Shanni nodded her agreement.

'That's a fine idea. Go right ahead.'

Okay, but he wasn't feeding them where he sat. This was a serious business. Carefully Harry wrapped up his pile of cooling chips, pushed himself awkwardly to his feet and stumped down to the water's edge. Then he laid the parcel on the wet sand, just as carefully unwrapped it and started tossing chips one at a time skyward but back toward the adults.

The gulls screamed in from everywhere, forming a cacophony of sound and movement between adults and child. A barrier... It was as if that was what Harry had meant to happen.

And for a long moment Nick watched, his heart doing all sorts of strange wrenching. Remembering just how hard his lessons of solitude had been to learn...

'They're planning on doing psychological assessment on him,' Shanni said conversationally, and Nick somehow hauled himself back to the present.

Psychological assessment... 'Because of the hostage thing?'

'No.' She shook her head. 'Because of before. And how he is now.'

'I don't understand.'

'This is as good as it gets,' she said sadly. 'He's as happy as he can be right now. I'm trying so hard, and so is Wendy, the head of his children's home. But he's so withdrawn. Around most people he dives for cover, or, if they come close, he screams blue murder. Screams and screams and screams. Wendy says he has night terrors and he's keeping every child in the home awake half the night.'

'So?'

'So if we don't get through to him then he'll be placed in a psychiatric institution. Wendy can't cope—and who can blame her? She's running a group home for children at risk and she has more than Harry to care for. They've tried foster homes but he doesn't last more than a night. Adoption's out of the question like he is now. We *must* get through to him.'

We...

'You mean...' Nick stirred a whirl of sand under his fingers. 'You mean *you*. And Wendy.'

She flicked a glance at him. 'Of course.' She shrugged. 'I mean me and Wendy.'

'If you don't mind me saying this,' he said softly, 'I don't see any professional detachment in this.'

'Professional detachment?'

'Surely your role of kindergarten teacher doesn't include mental health therapy for your students.'

Silence.

'He's not your responsibility,' Nick went on. There was no easy way to say this but it must be said. 'If Harry needs professional help, then surely a psychiatric institution is the place where he'll get it.'

'He needs to be loved.'

'Then he needs to be cured and then adopted.'

'Oh, sure,' she said, jeering. 'Cured and then adopted. But it's a Catch 22 situation, isn't it, Mr Daniels? He can't be adopted until he's cured and he can't be cured until he's adopted.'

'That sounds clever.'

'It's not.' She got up, her colour heightened so her cheeks were turning to rose, and there was anger building. Her eyes flashed fire and...contempt? 'Of course it's not simple, either,' she flashed at him. 'But I've no intention of talking smart or simple theories. I'm talking about a little boy's life. If I could, then I'd take him home with me. Maybe I'd have a chance to make a difference, but he doesn't want a woman. He needs a man to attach to. Everyone says that.'

'This is ridiculous. It's not your job to worry about it.'

'Of course it's not my job. It's no one's job, but at least I try. At least I care. Not like some people who say they live on stupid mountains!'

'I might as well do,' he snapped, stung. He rose to face her, fire meeting fire. Her anger was palpable—and so was his. How dared she throw this at him!

'Meaning?'

'Meaning, no, of course I don't want to get involved,' he threw back at her. 'Because what good would it do? You think I should try to form an attachment and then move away? You know as well as I do that it'd make everything worse.'

'Nick, you could do a lot of good in two years,' she said, softening as if there really was a chance she could persuade him.

'You're kidding.'

'No, you could,' she said urgently. 'Mary says you're bored with work already. The orphanage system runs a big-brother scheme. Just picking a child up from individual homes, taking him out, doing this sort of thing. Mucking around in the sun. Being a friend.'

'I wouldn't know the first thing about being a friend to a three-year-old.'

'I'll teach you,' she said. 'Wendy and I both think he's desperate for male contact. He and his dad were so close, and any female contact he had was appalling. He needs to bond with a male.'

'You *have* to be kidding!' He was facing her square on, and he couldn't believe this was happening. She was almost pleading—but not quite. Her eyes defied him to do this thing. They told him that this was his duty as another human—or the sort of human with any decency at all.

The sort with any love...

But any love had been kicked out of Nick Daniels a long time ago. He stared down into her blazing eyes and the feeling that grew in his heart was leaden and grey. What she was asking was impossible.

'No,' he said flatly, and took a step back. 'You don't know what you're asking.'

She opened her mouth to retort—and then shut it again. Once again there was that look—the look that said she saw further than words. And something changed. In that instant, anger moved to concern.

'What's happened to you, Nick?' she said softly, almost whispering into the soft wind. 'What's put you on top of that mountain?'

'I don't...'

'You don't want to talk about it. I can see that.' She smiled suddenly, tension dissolving as if it had never been. She even managed a wavering smile. 'Hmm. The plot thickens.'

'The plot...'

'Why you won't take your stupid tie off and you keep

combing your hair so you look like a city lawyer—even when it's totally inappropriate. What harm's a bit of ruffled hair? You might look like a sleek city lawyer in the city, but here your image just makes you look like Mafioso. And you don't know One, Two, Three, Jump...'

'Shanni...'

'Yes?' Amazingly there was a twinkle dancing back into her eyes.

'Butt out.'

'Nope.' She grinned. 'It's not my style. I'll back off, though,' she said equably. 'I can see a bit clearer what I'm fighting now. So I'll back off. But butt out? Never!'

There was still time left before three. Nick's idea of backing off was to retire quietly to his chambers. Shanni's idea of backing off was to head to the playground.

It was two against one and the outcome was never in doubt.

'I would like to go on the roundabout,' Harry said wistfully, looking at a platform mounted on springs, with four seats made to look like bucking horses. The idea was to sit on a horse and sway as you spun. The sight made Nick's stomach churn, especially after all those chips...

'That's another fine idea,' Shanni said roundly, fixing Nick with a look that defied him to refuse the child. 'Hop right up.'

But suddenly Harry wasn't so sure.

'It's high.'

'Nick will help you on—won't you, Nick?'

Oh, of course! He was getting almost past argument. So he hopped up onto the platform and lifted Harry onto a horse—and then, before he knew what she was about, the platform started to spin. Shanni, devilment in her eyes, had started to push.

'Hey...' He clutched the handle-cum-bridle, his hands over Harry's small ones, and held on for dear life. 'Stop!'

'It's okay, Nick! I can spin you both.' She was using both hands, running, shoving the platform around into free whirl. Her hair was flying, there was mischief sparking in her eyes and she was laughing up at both of them. 'Hold on, Harry!'

Hold on, Harry? What about *him*? 'Shanni, let me off.'

'You won't fall if you hold on,' Harry said kindly. And then, as the platform sped up, he threw back his head and smiled shyly up at Nick. 'This is fun!'

Fun!

But Harry's smile was infectious—and so was the way Shanni was laughing at them as she spun them around and around and around. He was way out of control and this woman had him so mesmerised there wasn't a thing he could do about it. 'I've been set up,' he managed weakly. 'You machiavellian...'

'Drat, you've found my true nature.' She chortled and ran on. 'There's nothing for it but to spin you faster. And faster and faster and faster...'

She did just that. Nick held on, standing above Harry and, whether he realised it or not, he was playing the protector. Because Harry was holding on as if his life depended on it, he was spinning and spinning, but *his* Nick was right above him and he knew his Nick wouldn't let him fall.

And suddenly it was...magic? The sun shone warmly down on their heads. The waves washed in and out on the beach below them. They spun and they spun, and Shanni pushed and ran and pushed and smiled...and watched both these males.

And she wondered...

'Shanni!'

It couldn't last. Fifteen minutes pushing was surely enough for any child—and Nick was all set to lose his chips!—but somehow he'd quelled his protests and it wasn't Harry who stopped them. The yell came from the road, and Nick looked over to find Shanni's John heading straight for them.

Good old dependable John, Nick thought wryly, watching him hurrying across the sand-hills as they spun. The look on his face said he was here to save his Shanni from any danger. But from which of them? From the psychotic three-year-old or the slick city lawyer?

John must have decided it was fate worse than death for Shanni to be stuck with such a combination, Nick thought humourlessly. Little did John know his beloved had engineered the whole thing—including stranding him on this devilish platform. It was Nick who needed saving!

But John only had eyes for Shanni. No matter. John was welcome to save Shanni all he liked, Nick decided, but then he felt bitterness behind the thought—and the sensation jolted him.

What on earth did he have to be bitter about? he demanded incredulously of himself. This girl was nothing to do with him, and neither was the man she intended to marry.

'Shanni…love…'

The roundabout slowed as Shanni's attention was distracted. Thank heaven… Nick abandoned his horse, staggered off, lurched as his feet hit solid earth and then tried to stop his world from falling right over.

Good grief… And Harry was looking at him as if he was wondering why Nick had climbed off!

'John.' Shanni had smiled a welcome as John strode across the sand-hills, but Nick heard a note of wariness enter her voice. As if she wasn't sure what to expect…

'Mary told me you'd be here.' John was out of breath, as though he'd been hurrying for much longer than the time it had taken to stride across the sand-hills. He sounded aggrieved. 'I thought you were checking bathroom tiles on your afternoon off.'

'Nope.' Shanni shrugged and kept her smile fixed. 'You told me I should check tiles, but I don't see the point when we haven't decided on a house plan.' She smiled placatingly and then tried to extend the conversation. 'John, you remember Nick?'

'Of course I remember Nick,' John said grumpily, digging his hands deep in his pockets. He flicked an acknowledging nod at the staggering Nick and went straight back to his grievance. Which was just as well, because Nick was in no state to greet him. 'So why weren't you at the tile place? I decided to leave the hay and come in and meet you.'

'Push,' said Harry. 'Nick, why are you off?'

'Too much of a good thing,' Nick gasped. He waved a helpless hand at Shanni, who was looking suspiciously as if she might laugh at his plight. She'd better not! 'But go right ahead without me. Shanni, push!'

'Wuss!' But she pushed, grinning at him without sympathy and then turning back to John as she pushed.

'John, it might rain tomorrow,' she said thoughtfully, still pushing. Harry gave Nick a look of disgust—Wimpy adults! his look said—but then decided he'd turn his attention to the sea, as if he was looking for pirates.

'The hay will spoil if it rains,' Shanni said.

'That's why I don't understand why you're not where you said you would be,' John snapped. 'I don't want to waste time.'

'So…you were coming to choose tiles—or check on me?'

'I just wanted to see that you were okay.'

'That's really nice of you, John,' she said softly. 'But, as you can see, I'm fine. Choosing tiles or eating lunch on the beach are hardly dangerous occupations. Don't let the hay spoil on my account.'

'Why are you here—with him?' He glared at Nick and

Nick raised his eyebrows and smiled politely. Or tried to smile politely. His whole world was still looking decidedly crooked.

He said nothing. One reason was that he knew when to shut up, but the second was that he was still concentrating on balance. Very important, balance! He wondered how it would look if he lay down.

He didn't. A man had some pride! Plus the sand was wobbling.

'Nick and I are taking Harry out to lunch.' Shanni was smiling at Harry, who was still looking for pirates. Great! They were welcome to pay attention to anything other than Nick's condition! 'This is John, Harry. You want to say hello?'

'No,' said Harry, and Nick didn't blame him.

But he was still spinning! 'Don't you want to stop yet?' Nick demanded.

'No,' said Harry, very definitely. 'If you pushed as well I could go faster.'

Good grief! But there was no alternative. Clutching his balance and pride together, Nick managed a sickly shrug. He pushed.

And he listened.

'Shanni, let's go,' John was saying urgently. 'If you come with me now we still have enough time to choose tiles.'

'That's crazy,' Shanni said, exasperated. 'We don't even have the house plan.' She took a deep breath. 'In fact, we haven't even decided to get married.'

That floored John. 'Of course we're getting married.'

'You haven't actually asked me.'

'We talked about it the other day. And we always knew...'

'John, we need to talk about this by ourselves,' she said

urgently, casting a sideways glance at Nick—who just as carefully looked away. 'Maybe we could meet tonight.'

But John had no intention of being placated. 'This is ridiculous. I came into town to choose tiles.'

'I'm with Harry. And Nick.'

'Leave the kid with the lawyer.'

'Hey...' Nick's protest was involuntary—but unnecessary. He could safely leave this to Shanni. She was angry enough for both of them.

'The *kid's* name is Harry,' she said bluntly. 'Not "the kid". And Harry is my friend. I invited him and Nick—who's a magistrate, not just a lawyer—out to lunch and for a play in the playground. When we're finished—and not before—I'll take Harry back to Wendy.'

'Wendy...' John's voice rose in incredulity. 'You mean this is a kid from the *orphanage*?'

'Yes,' she said, and there was ice dripping from the word. Back off, Nick was thinking urgently, but there was no way he could get that message across. John had no intention of backing off. This was a man used to getting his own way, and he wasn't tuned in to ice.

'Shanni, this is ridiculous,' John said through gritted teeth. 'The whole town saw you walking down the street with this guy, and with the kid between you. Malcolm Taylor rang to tell me...'

'So this is the real reason you're here?' Shanni's anger was building by the minute. 'Because Malcolm saw me with another man and decided to report me?'

'The town will think you're two-timing me!'

'By sitting on the beach eating fish and chips with the local magistrate? In broad daylight and with a child between us?' Nick and Harry were forgotten now. If he were John he'd disappear for a while, Nick thought. He could feel the anger radiating from Shanni, and it was almost tangible.

'It's not his place to take you to lunch.'

'*He* didn't take me to lunch. I took *him* for lunch.'

'It's true,' Nick said mildly. 'I had no choice at all. Ask Harry. I don't have a choice in anything. This lady has the force of two bulldozers.'

He was ignored.

'Look, come and choose tiles and we'll forget all about this,' John said urgently. 'I mean…the town will forget…'

'That I'm a two-timing hussy?'

'I never said…'

'You didn't need to.' She was fairly spitting. 'John, I like you very much, and you've been a real friend—but I will not be *owned*.'

'You mean you don't want to marry me?'

She paused. There was a long, long silence. Unnoticed, the roundabout slowed to a halt. Both Nick and Harry were watching, entranced. Pirates and stomachs forgotten.

'I guess…' She closed her eyes and when she opened them the determination that Nick was starting to know was back in force. 'I guess that's what I do mean, John. Thank you for asking, but no.'

'You're kidding!'

'No. I'm sorry.'

'I see.' Once again, there was a long, long silence—and then John turned to Nick, and the look he cast him was pure malevolence. 'I just hope to hell he's worth it,' he spat. 'To throw me over for a bloody lawyer with designer suits…'

And he turned and stalked off over the sand-hills.

'Push,' said Harry.

That at least was something he could do. Nick pushed while Shanni gazed at the retreating back of her lover and he could see indecision written all over her.

'Go after him,' he said gently. 'I can take care of Harry.'

What was he saying?

'Thank you.' She turned to face them, an overbright smile pinned to her face. The decision had been made and there wasn't regret there as far as Nick could see. There was just pure anger. 'But I don't need any more males telling me what to do.'

'Especially not a designer-suited lawyer?'

It broke the ice. She stared at him for a long minute and then, slowly, the anger faded. 'Oh, heck…' She broke into a weak chuckle. 'Oh, help. I'm sorry. No. Wasn't he awful?'

'But…if people are getting that impression…' Another thought was hitting Nick with force now, and he didn't like it. If the town thought Shanni was throwing her John over for him… 'Maybe we should cool it.'

She stared. And then her jaw dropped in a sardonic look of incredulity. 'Cool it? Cool *what*?'

'I don't know. Maybe John has a point.'

Anger was flooding right back. 'So people all over town think I'm falling for you because I asked you to lunch. *And you're worried about it?* You jerk! You're as conceited and pompous as John.'

'Push,' said Harry firmly—he was tired of this adult conversation and was back to basics—and they both pushed while undercurrents zoomed around and between them as if the playground was wired for electricity. And some of it had got loose.

'I'm sorry,' Nick said after a bit. Maybe he had overreacted. It was just this small-town thing. He did not want to get involved. He glanced at his watch and saw with relief there was just fifteen minutes left before three. 'I need to get back.'

'Of course you do,' she said cordially. 'Don't let me keep you.'

'You're not coming?'

'Harry and I are playing on the roundabout,' she snapped. 'You do what you like.'

'Right. Right, then.'

He took a deep breath, looked at her for a long minute and nodded.

'See you later, Harry,' he said.

'When?' Harry demanded, startled. His voice was urgent. 'When will you see me?'

'I'm not sure.'

'Mr Daniels is a very busy man,' Shanni said icily. 'He's probably got tiles to buy.'

'I do have a court case or two to judge.'

'Then don't let us keep you,' she said through gritted teeth. 'Harry and I can manage very well without you. We can manage without men in general and without two males in particular. And one of them's you.'

'What's been happening?'

'I was expecting you to come back with a black eye at least.'

Nick was no sooner in the courthouse than he was pounced on. Mary was at her desk, agog, and Rob was standing beside her, immaculate in his police uniform. The physical likeness to Shanni was unmistakable—as was their ability to ignore his personal boundaries.

He stared at both of them with dislike. There was sand in his shoes. He needed time to empty it before he was due in court in four minutes. His stomach was still churning from the roundabout and he felt ill. He didn't need an inquisition.

'Why are you here?' he snapped at Rob.

'Hey, I brought the prisoner,' Rob said, aggrieved. 'Not that there's any need for force. It's Bart Commin in for shoplifting. He pinches four cans of baked beans every second Wednesday, because that's the day before pension. It

drives everyone nuts, but as soon as we make it official—
try to give him the beans and dock his pension—he changes
stores. We figure he likes the excitement.'

'Great.' Nick groaned. 'Fourteen years' intellectual training for this.'

'Your tie's crooked,' Mary said, bright-eyed and interested. 'You've never had a crooked tie before.'

'So your sister had her wicked way with me behind the
sand-hills,' Nick snarled. 'You want to put a two-page announcement in the local paper?'

'Don't reckon we have to,' Rob said lazily, and grinned.
'John's done it for us.'

Nick stared. 'What exactly do you mean by that?'

'He's spreading it all over town,' Rob told him. 'I've
heard it from at least three people on the way here. Seems
my sister's thrown John over for the magistrate.'

'Oh, great!'

'Your hair's not mussed,' Mary said, in a tone saying
she wouldn't have minded if it was. 'That means you can't
have been too far out of line.'

'Plus they had the littl'un with them,' Rob agreed. 'It
wouldn't have happened.'

'You'll go far as a policeman,' Nick snapped. 'Great
detective work. Do you mind? I have a court case to run.'

'Bart won't worry if you're running late,' Rob said easily. 'I'm prosecuting and he's defending himself. There's
hardly an army of lawyers waiting.'

'No.' He would have preferred it if there was—in fact
he would have preferred anything to these four enquiring
eyes.

'Did she really throw John over?' Mary asked, breath-
less.

He guessed he could tell them that. 'She did.'

There was a long drawn-out sigh from the pair of them,
and he looked on, bemused.

'Do you mind telling me what's going on?'

'We can't stand the man,' Rob said simply. 'None of us can. We were starting to worry she'd marry him through lack of competition.'

'And now along you come,' Mary said dreamily.

'Rob?' Nick eyed his arresting officer with disfavour.

'Yes, sir?' There was a glint in Rob's eye that reminded Nick of Shanni, and he wasn't sure he liked it. He wasn't the least bit sure he wasn't being laughed at here.

'There's a jug of water on my bench. Fetch it and throw it over your sister.'

'If you say so.' Rob grinned and Mary stopped looking dreamy and gave a half-hearted chuckle herself.

'Okay. I know I'm being stupid. It's just... I mean you're eligible as anything, and you'd be quite good-looking if you didn't have the...' She paused and Nick glowered.

'If I didn't have the what?'

'Pot-belly and bald spot?' Rob suggested, and hooted with laughter. 'Jeepers, Mary, leave the guy alone.' But Mary just looked helpful.

'It's your hairstyle and slick clothes,' she said. 'They make you look like a gangster.'

'Gee, thanks.'

'Or one of those smart city lawyers you see on the movies,' she added. 'And you're not one of those.'

'No. More's the pity.'

'You don't mind me saying it?'

'Why should I?' He rolled his eyes. 'Go ahead. Any more improvements you can think of while you're at it?'

'You don't really have to wear those skinny ties,' she ventured.

'The suit doesn't fit here,' Rob added, joining right into the spirit of things. 'Old Judge Andrews wore tweed.'

'The old judge kept forgetting to take his wellingtons off, too,' Mary said thoughtfully. 'He had a hobby farm so he kept arriving in court smelling of cow dung. It made him…I don't know…more approachable somehow.'

'You'd like me to come to court without my hair combed, in a tweed jacket, a wide tie and stinking of cow dung?'

'You have to do something. You'll never win our Shanni like you are now.' Rob chortled at Nick's expression and threw up his hands in mock surrender. 'Okay, Your Worship. I can see I've gone too far. Let me organise a prisoner for you and we'll get this court case under way.'

He shouldn't worry.

He shouldn't give a damn what they all thought of him, Nick decided as the afternoon wore on. The cases were trivial and demanded hardly any thought at all. He might as well think of his appearance.

He might as well think about Shanni.

Which was really, really stupid.

He'd go up to town this weekend, he decided. If he left by five tomorrow night he could be back in his inner-city apartment by nine. Maybe ring a couple of friends, catch a late show, see the latest Enrico exhibition on Saturday…

'Four hundred dollars or ten days in custody,' he said, and discovered the whole courtroom was looking at him.

'But…' It was Mary, and she bit her lip almost as soon as she said it.

'What?'

'Fifty bucks or overnight,' the defendant explained for her, in a voice that sounded like gravel. The old man was an alcoholic. He stank. The smell of him reached every corner of the court.

'Overnight gives us time to see he's fed and washed,' Rob explained.

'So ten days gives you longer. Next case…'

And he closed his file and glared at them all. And they glared right back. Every single one of them.

And Shanni was waiting for him when court was finished for the day. Her anger was still sky-high. He came out of court, tossed his gown aside and turned to find Shanni watching him from the corridor.

'I suppose you know what you've done,' she said bluntly.

Nick sighed. Now what?

'Let's see,' he said wearily. 'According to town gossip, so far today I've ravished you over fish and chips, I've had my wicked way in the sand-hills, I've broken your engagement to your knight in shining armour, and I've smashed the unwritten dress code for Bay Beach court. What else is there left?'

'You've made Emma feed Bart for ten days!'

'Emma?'

'Rob's wife. She does the meals for the custody cells. And Bart'll dry out. We'll have him screaming the place down.'

'Then maybe he needs to be dried out.' This was none of her business.

'I thought Mary warned you. Bart's dried out at least fifty times in living memory, all of them in the police cells, all of them with Rob and Emma not getting sleep for days and all of them totally useless as he hits the bottle the minute he's back on the town. But go ahead. Jail him.'

'I already have.'

'I know.' She gritted her teeth. 'Smart city lawyers...'

'I *am* the magistrate,' he said mildly, and she ground her teeth some more.

'Yeah. Well, stop filling police cells and go do something useful.'

Something useful… For heaven's sake, hadn't these people heard of a little respect? *He was the magistrate!*

But respect wasn't in Shanni's vocabulary.

'The psychologist is coming to the children's home tomorrow to assess Harry,' she continued. 'That's why I'm here. Don't get any funny ideas that I might want to see you or anything. I don't. But Wendy needs a statement saying that you've been able to make contact.'

'Make contact?' Nick stared, bemused. She was still furious and she looked really something when she was angry. As if there were sparks inside as well as out.

'Yes. That you've been able to communicate with him and he's showed signs of affection. Otherwise he risks being classified as autistic and we'll get nowhere. He'll be taken away from Wendy, and there's no chance he'll be considered for adoption with a label like that.'

'Shanni, it's…'

'None of your business,' she snapped, eyes flashing. 'Like Bart isn't my business. This is a small community here, Nick Daniels, and everyone cares for everybody. And even if it wasn't a small community… Haven't you ever heard the line "Any man's *death* diminishes *me*…"'

That floored him. For heaven's sake… John Donne's poetry being flung at him by angry kindergarten teachers…

'Any man's *death* diminishes *me*, because I am involved in *Mankind*…'

But Nick wasn't, he thought blankly. No way. He'd tried as hard as he could, for all of his life, to be exactly the opposite. As uninvolved in mankind as possible.

'How can you not care?' Shanni said hotly. 'Nick, you're the only hope he has.'

'I…'

'You don't care for anyone. Of course you don't. I can see that.' She shook her blonde curls in fury. 'So don't do anything about it. See him locked in a psychiatric institution…'

'Hey…'

'If you care, then go and talk to Wendy.'

'Wendy?'

'Wendy,' she said kindly, as if he was a sandwich short of a picnic. 'The head of the children's home he's in. Bay Beach orphanage is split into five homes and Wendy's in charge of Harry's.' She glared again. 'So help her. If you have one ounce of decency in your body then it's the least you can do.'

'But you…'

'And you needn't worry. You won't meet me there, so your reputation will remain untarnished. I'm going to a movie with my mother. Something about a runaway bride.' She glowered. 'Which will suit me down to the ground. Runaway bride? Ha! If all the men around her are as appalling as you and John, I can't say I blame her for her choice.'

CHAPTER FIVE

GREAT!

He seemed to have sand everywhere. Nick took himself back up to his apartment, emptied his shoes, washed his face and poured himself a glass of wine. It didn't work. He still felt gritty and unsettled.

And like a king-sized rat.

He made himself steak and salad, sat down to watch the news on TV and he still felt rat-like. Which was stupidly unfair.

Finally he showered and changed every piece of his sand-impregnated clothing, donning casual trousers and an open-necked shirt. Then he stared at himself in the mirror. See? he demanded of no one in particular—or the absent Shanni. He could be casual if he wanted to be.

The thought was so pathetic and inane he made himself grin.

His hair needed attention. He'd washed the sand out, and it was drying as its usual mop of unruly black curls. This wasn't a judge-look at all. He grimaced, started to comb it flat and smooth—and then he stopped.

This was stupid, he conceded. Slick hairstyles for casual was stupid. He wasn't dressing for anyone. He'd leave it be—just run a comb loosely through it and leave it. Just for tonight.

After all, he was only reading legal briefs tonight—wasn't he? Hardly worth donning his city lawyer image for.

He read one legal brief and paused.

Harry... Psychiatric assessment tomorrow.

Harry...

It was nothing to do with him, he thought savagely—desperately. He couldn't help.

But in his heart, maybe he knew he could.

He'd heard court cases before, submissions of social workers on why a child should be sent home to his parents or fostered or sent to a remand home. *This child is incapable of attachment. Borderline autism. There's no point in attempting foster care. We believe institutional care is the only option.*

Harry was only three years old and, if Shanni was right...if he *could* help...

Nick was in a position to guess that attachment was possible if they found a home where there was a decent male parent. Harry just needed his dad, Nick thought.

As he had.

That had nothing to do with it, he thought savagely. His own background was irrelevant. Think of practicalities. He shook off the feeling of wanting to stay right out of this and let himself remember how Harry had felt holding him close. He'd hugged him all that long night of the hostage drama, and it hadn't just been Harry who'd received comfort.

This was ridiculous!

Yes, but just talking to Wendy couldn't hurt—telling Wendy if she wanted a statement then he was prepared to make it. It couldn't hurt to do that much—and then steer clear. And...Shanni was at the movies.

It was only nine. Not too late. Decision made, he grabbed his jacket and headed for the door.

With his hair still tousled.

'If it'll help then I'll put that all in writing.'

'It will.' Wendy stared across the table at her visitor, her eyes troubled. 'The only problem is...'

'Mmm?'

'You're saying he shouldn't be institutionalised because he's capable of attachment. But you're not willing to allow that attachment.'

'I...no.'

'Do you know about our big brother scheme?'

'Shanni...Miss McDonald told me about it, yes.'

'And you're not willing to be a part of it?'

'No.'

'Hmm.' She paused and regarded him across the table with knowing eyes. In silence.

Which Nick found vaguely unsettling. The woman was still relatively young, close to thirty, maybe, but Nick knew instinctively that she'd make a great house mother for troubled kids. She was sort of...comfortable. She had kindly eyes that crinkled from too much smiling—eyes that said she accepted all comers as she found them.

And she knew what she was seeing now. 'You've had a tough time yourself,' she said softly, and Nick stared.

'How...?'

'How do I know?' She spread her hands. 'You get to know the look. And Shanni told me.

'What on earth does Shanni know?'

'She sees as much as I do.' Wendy smiled and pushed her fingers through her mass of dark curls. She'd tied them back into a knot but they were breaking free everywhere. 'She's quite a girl. If that's all, then...'

'Is Harry asleep?' Now, why had he asked that?

'I doubt it.' She hesitated. 'It's hard to get him to sleep. He lies there for hours, just staring into the dark. But if you're not willing to take this further then maybe it's not such a good idea to prolong the agony.'

'The agony?'

'Harry wants you,' she said simply. 'He cries to go to you. That's why Shanni took him to lunch with you today.' And then she paused as she heard a car pull up outside.

There was a click of the gate, and then a low laugh as someone greeted one of the older children. 'Speaking of which...here she is.'

The first thing she saw was his hair.

Shanni burst in the door and stopped dead. She'd never expected that Nick would come. She'd been expecting Wendy, and Wendy was there, but so was Nick and this was a very different Nick. So far she'd seen him groomed and immaculate and slick and smooth. Now...he was in casual trousers, a short-sleeved, open-necked shirt and his hair was tousled and thick and unruly.

She could see why he combed it down. Smoothed, it looked like the hairstyle of a barrister of the highest standing. Now it was a tousled mop, and he looked years younger. He didn't look like a magistrate, she thought. He looked...nice.

Nick wasn't nice, she told herself, strangely off-balance. He was a toad. All men were toads. John was toad number one but Nick was running a close second.

'How was the movie?' he asked mildly, and she wrinkled her nose in distaste.

'Lousy.'

'How come?' Wendy smiled and rose to fetch more coffee. 'Weren't you seeing the one about the runaway bride?'

'Yes—but it had a stupid ending. She didn't keep running.'

Wendy choked on laughter, then crossed to give her friend a hug. They were obviously very close. 'Hey, it's okay. Maybe you and John can sort it out.'

'No, we can't,' Shanni said darkly, hugging back. 'He wants a den.'

'What's wrong with a man wanting a den?' Nick asked, startled, and got a glower for his pains.

'We did house plans last night,' she explained—as if he

was a simpleton. 'John has it all worked out. Three bedrooms, living room, kitchen for me and a den for him. Isn't that cosy?'

'A man needs a den,' Nick said, and found he now had two women glaring at him. Oh, help...

'I have a den,' said Wendy.

'Why can't I have a den?' demanded Shanni. 'Chauvinist twit. But when I said that, John just laughed—like I was being cute because what would the little woman want a den for? And then he told me to go and choose bathroom tiles. And then today...'

'I know what happened today,' Wendy said, and both of them stared at her.

'Well, if you will have your domestics in full view of the pier... Half the retired folk of the town listened in.'

'Oh, great.' Nick groaned.

'I don't know why you're complaining,' Shanni said crossly. 'You get to play magistrate for two years and then leave this place. I'm stuck here for ever.' She helped herself from the coffee pot Wendy produced, sat down and stuck a thumb in the direction of Nick. 'What's he doing here?'

'Refusing to play big brother.'

'Hey, I'm signing an affidavit like Shanni wanted me to,' Nick said, stung. 'What else do you want?'

'You to go in and hug Harry goodnight—and promise you'll do the same tomorrow,' Wendy said promptly.

Silence.

'See,' Shanni said morosely into her coffee. 'They're all useless.'

'There's reasons he's like this,' Wendy said kindly. 'He's got a past.'

'Yeah, but if he had real courage...'

'Are we talking about me, here,' Nick said carefully. 'If we are, then would you mind including me?'

'You don't include anyone else,' Shanni retorted. 'You

go on being solitary and we'll go on not communicating. That's the way you like it.'

'Shanni…'

'If I communicate with him he accuses me of setting my cap at him,' she told Wendy, ignoring him nicely. 'As if I would. The heroine in my movie had the right idea—but to give in at the end and marry one of the species… No!'

'I reckon you ought to try, though,' Wendy said thoughtfully. 'Communicating, I mean. Now he's abandoned his smooth look he seems sort of cute.'

This was way out of hand. He was getting out of here—fast.

'He is cute,' Shanni admitted. 'But ego…lawyer and judge and good looks combined. Phew!'

'And aloof,' Wendy said sadly. 'Puts himself above everyone in this place. Bet he thinks he's the greatest intellectual in town.'

'Hey…'

'Bet he never ever stays for weekends,' Wendy said. 'What's the bet he's getting in his cute little car tomorrow and heading back to Melbourne for the weekend just as fast as he can drive? Because this place threatens him.'

'Mmm.' Shanni nodded. 'I can't say I blame him.'

'Shanni!' Wendy stared. 'Hey, keep your end of the conversation going here, girl. I can't keep lawyer-bashing on my own.'

'But it does get a bit claustrophobic.' Shanni was no longer looking at Nick. She was staring into the dregs of her coffee, her mind on her own problems. 'We're having a family beach picnic on Sunday,' she explained morosely. 'Grandpa's seventieth birthday. They'll be so sympathetic—or secretly pleased, which is worse.'

'Because of you and John.'

'The whole town thought we were getting married. Including John.'

'Including you?' Wendy prodded, and Shanni shrugged.

'Yeah, I guess…'

'So take your new fella.'

'I don't have a new fella.' Shanni thumped her mug on the table. 'Wendy, will you stop it? Everyone thinks Nick and I ran straight into each other's arms, and the last thing I need is yet another man.'

'What about you?' Wendy said, wheeling to Nick and honing in like an arrow. 'Interested?'

'No!'

'There you go, then,' she said, and sat back smugly, arms folded. 'So neither of you are interested in any sort of relationship, but both of you are interested in saving Harry. So therefore…'

'Therefore…' Nick was being swept away here. This woman was too much for him. He was glad she didn't have a legal degree, he thought. She'd wipe the floor with him at the bar.

'So therefore I can tell the assessor tomorrow that Harry's developing relationships all over the place, and I can tell Harry that the two of you are taking him out on Sunday to Shanni's family picnic.'

'No!' they said in unison, and Wendy grinned at the twin sound of revulsion in their voices.

'Why not? It means I have a promise I can use to put Harry to sleep at night. It'll give me breathing space. If I can use the two of you 'til he relaxes with me…'

'Wendy…'

'Look!' She was all earnestness now, fighting for one of her kids, and Nick knew his first assessment of her had been right. She'd give her all to make sure the kids she cared for had a chance. 'I can't cope with Harry, now,' she admitted. 'He screams and he won't let me near. I beg, cajole, hug, threaten, but nothing I say makes any difference. But if I say, "You go to bed on time and you eat your dinner and you don't scream the place down, then Shanni and Nick will take you out on a picnic on Sunday…'''

'I'm going back to Melbourne,' Nick said faintly.

'So what's more important?' Wendy was fighting every way she knew how. 'Your weekend in Melbourne? Or a little boy's future? If I can settle him here, make the psychologist see that there's a chance he might settle…'

'Wendy, we're not promising anything long-term,' Shanni said uneasily. 'I mean, if he grows too attached…'

'You tried to talk Nick into being big brother to him,' Wendy said sternly. 'Anyone can see Nick won't buy that sort of responsibility on his own—he's running scared—so maybe you can convince him to share. Instead of a big brother—why not brother and sister? What could be simpler than that?'

'Maybe…' Shanni was dubious.

'And it's even neutral,' Wendy said triumphantly. 'No sex at all.'

'Or not in front of the children.' Shanni's irrepressible twinkle peeped out, and Nick groaned. Heck, this was his weekend they were talking about. This was stupid. There was no chance he was staying.

And then the door opened and a small face appeared, peering around as if he expected to be knocked back again. Harry was wearing pyjamas a couple of sizes too big for him, his fibreglass cast made them look ungainly and awkward, and his eyes were way too big for his face.

'My Nick's here,' he whispered, unbelieving, and Nick's heart jerked with pain.

'You should be in bed, young man,' Wendy said, crossing to scoop him up in her arms. He held himself rigid, arching back in a pose of rejection that Nick was starting to know.

'Why is Nick here?' he whispered.

'He came to invite you to lunch on Sunday. Would you like to go?'

Harry's eyes swung to Nick's. His face said he didn't believe a word.

'It's true,' Nick said weakly, because there was nothing else to say. 'Sunday picnic. With Miss McDonald for her grandpa's birthday.'

'Shanni,' said Shanni. 'You can call me Shanni when we're not at kindergarten. Would you like to come to the beach with us again, Harry?'

'Yes.' It was one simple word—but it was almost like a sigh of relief.

'Then you have to promise to go straight to sleep, Harry, lad,' Wendy said sternly. 'Three more sleeps until Sunday and no protests.'

'Three more sleeps—and then you'll come?' He was looking straight at Nick, his eyes searching for the truth.

'I...yes.'

'Would you like to tuck him back into bed?' Wendy asked gently, and proffered the small body toward Nick

Nick froze.

But they were all looking at him. Wendy. Harry. And Shanni. He was on some sort of fence, he thought. One way was safety—the way he knew. The other—the other was the unknown, and the unknown scared the life out of him.

But still they looked at him, and Harry's eyes said he expected nothing. Life had slapped him once too often to believe in happy endings. And he couldn't bear it.

'Okay, kid,' Nick said resignedly, and rose and accepted Harry from Wendy's arms. Harry's arms swept around his neck and clung. 'Where's your bed? Show me.'

*   *   *

'He's gorgeous.'

'You said that about John.' Shanni poured herself more coffee and sank down opposite her friend.

'I lied. John's a meat-head. Pleasant, kind, but a bit…you know—the lights are on but no one's home.'

'And this guy?'

'The lights are off and the door's locked but he's home all right,' Wendy said. 'He's all in there but he's not letting it show. He's running scared.'

'I'm not exactly chasing him.' Shanni sighed. 'Heck, the last thing I want is emotional entanglement. Especially not with some smart-alec city lawyer.'

'Just one step at a time,' Wendy said gently. 'Just concentrate on Harry. But if you can kill two birds with one stone…'

'I don't know what you mean.'

'I mean that man in there has been badly hurt in the past,' Wendy said sternly. 'It stands out a mile. In my profession you know the look, and you can see it as well as me. I reckon our magistrate needs Harry as much as Harry needs him.'

'I hope you're right.' Shanni looked dubiously at her friend. 'And I hope he sees it.'

'I know I'm right,' Wendy said to herself later as she closed her door on the pair of them. 'I also think there are more needs here than Harry's—and I hope you're both wise enough to see it.'

Shanni intended walking.

Nick expected Shanni's car to be with his, but there was only his sports car parked outside.

'Mum dropped me off here,' Shanni told him. 'My car's got a cracked head, or something ghastly, and may be on its way to the car graveyard as we speak. The mechanics just shake their heads and groan every time I ask. So Mum drove me to the pictures, but I wanted to check on Harry afterwards. I'm walking home.'

'Where's home?'

'A mile or so thataway.'

'A mile!' Nick looked out into the dark in the direction she was pointing. They were on the outskirts of town, and the road she was pointing to led northwards, into the dark 'You can't do that!'

'Hey, this is Bay Beach,' she said, laughing. 'You don't get mugged in Bay Beach.'

'There are weirdos everywhere. Does your mother know you intend walking?'

'I told her I'd call a cab,' Shanni admitted. 'But I want to walk. I need to think.'

'You don't walk.'

'I'm a big girl now.'

'And I'm a criminal lawyer. A magistrate. I know what's out there.'

'Oh, scare me stupid, why don't you?' She shook her head, half-laughing, half-nervous. 'Cut it out.'

'Get in the car, Shanni,' he said heavily. He'd seen too much in this job to let anyone take stupid risks. Especially Shanni! 'Do your thinking when you're safe in your own bed. I'm taking you home.'

'I don't...'

'Shanni, please...'

She stared at him for a long moment, hearing the trace of fear in his voice—and then she silently climbed into his car.

She didn't know this man at all, she thought.

And she was almost fearful of the sensation.

Shanni's family farm was set back from the road, between the main road and the coast. The country was moonlit, and

Nick could see that it was magnificent—rolling hills, vast gum trees, and cattle standing peacefully in the moonlight.

'It's lovely,' he said, and she cast him a wry look.

'Hardly your cup of tea.'

'No.'

'Why did you come here?' she asked. They'd been silent all the way from town, but now, as the car pulled to a halt before the farmhouse verandah, she seemed to find her tongue.

'It's the first step to becoming a judge. I don't want to stay a lawyer for ever,' he said, and unexpectedly she grinned.

'Then you've taken the first step. You've stopped wearing your suit and tie. Congratulations.'

It was hard not to grin back. Her smile was infectious. 'It's back to suits tomorrow.'

'Magistrates don't need suits. They need...I don't know. Knowledge. Wisdom. Compassion.'

'Failing all that, suits will have to do.'

'Hmm.' She shook her head at him. He cut the engine— she should get out—but the night was still and warm and there was this thing between them that needed examining...

'It's a shame,' she said softly, 'to wear such severe suits, to flatten that gorgeous hair...' Then, before he could do anything to stop her, her hand came out and touched his head. She was running her fingers through his tousled curls as if she couldn't help herself. 'It's great hair. Lovely hair. Do you take after your mother or father?'

'I have no idea.' The feeling of her fingers in his hair was weird. It set every nerve in his body alight. He found himself clenching his hands on the steering wheel, staring out at the night beyond and trying to halt the flood of sensations coursing through his body.

'I see.' Silence. Then... 'So Wendy's right.'

'Wendy sticks her nose where it has no business being.' His voice sounded as strained as he felt.

'Maybe,' Shanni agreed. 'But, then, Wendy's like a judge. Knowledgeable. Wise. And kind. Like you intend to be.'

'I don't know about that.' He stirred and shifted his hands—and clenched them again on the wheel.

'Why don't you know your parents?'

He shrugged. 'I have vague memories of my mother. She had a different hair colour every time she visited me, though. Who can say if she looked like me?'

'You didn't live with her?'

'Not often. Mostly I lived in foster homes. She wouldn't let me be adopted.'

'Oh, Nick...'

'Heck, we're not feeling sorry for me, here,' he said savagely. It was a long time since he'd railed against the unfairness of his past. 'I've had a very good life, thank you very much. Some great foster homes.'

'Many?'

'A dozen or so. My mother kept arriving and deciding she'd take me back. For a week or so. Or she'd just make so much fuss the foster parents thought I was too much trouble.' He smiled without humour, staring out at the dark. 'My mother and I have a very low tolerance rate. Domesticity's not my scene.'

'Not your mother's scene?'

'As you say.'

'And now you're set to be a judge.'

'Great, isn't it? His voice was self-mocking. 'Back-street kid makes good.'

'You've fought for this?'

'Every way I know how,' he told her, and there was no way he could stop the icy determination from his voice. 'Every waking minute. I remember...'

'You remember what?' She was almost whispering.

And he told her. It must have been the night, he told himself later. The warmth of the evening, and the scent of the garden and the eucalypts towering over them with the stars glimmering through. Or...the warmth drifting between.

Or... It must have been that she was a listener—not like any other woman he'd gone out with. He only knew he had to talk—and talk of something he'd never talked about in his life before.

'I remember sitting in court,' he said, and he was speaking almost to himself, his voice half-mocking. 'I was about seven. I'd spent a month with my mother and the welfare authorities got an injunction to take me away. I was... neglected, to say the least. So they were all in court— my mother—her boyfriend—my mother's neighbours—social workers I'd never met before. And they all were saying what should happen to me.'

'So?' Her voice was gentle.

'So I remember looking up at the judge and he just said...he just said what would happen. No argument and it was the right thing. It was what I wanted, and it meant I got fed again and got to go to school. So I figured...right then and there I figured...that that was what I was going to be. Someone who could say what would happen.'

'Oh, Nick...'

'Pretty silly reason for wanting to be a judge, huh?' he said, still in that self-mocking voice. Good grief, he was pathetic.

But she didn't think so. Shanni was saying nothing, just sitting watching him with eyes that were almost luminescent in the dark. There was a glimmer on her lashes that could almost have been tears.

'Hey...'

'I think that's the best reason I've ever heard for wanting

to be a judge, Nick Daniels,' she said in a choked voice. 'And now you've made it.'

'I want high-court judge,' he said, and his voice firmed.

'Won't magistrate at Bay Beach do? Or county-court judge? Our last judge stayed thirty years.'

'Thirty years!' His tone told her what he thought of that. 'No chance. Two years and I'm out of here.'

'Country gets under your skin.' She couldn't stop a note of bitterness creeping into her own voice then. 'Though I'd have to agree that sometimes the place can even get to me.'

'Sometimes even you want to get away?'

'Sometimes,' she admitted. 'This week will be hard.'

'Because?'

'In case you haven't noticed,' she retorted, 'I threw away a perfectly good marriage proposition this afternoon. The news will be all over the town by now. John's a very nice person.'

'He's a stuffed shirt.'

She grinned at that. 'Yes. You see it. I see it now, too, but the town sees a very nice boy who I've thrown over for nothing. John will be getting sympathy and I'll get the Wicked Witch Of The West treatment. Apart from my family—who'll be so pleased that I'll want to slug them.'

'Why?'

'Do you enjoy people telling you, ''I told you so''?' she demanded bitterly. 'No? Neither do I. My family saw the stuffed shirt bit before I did.' Then she paused as, up on the verandah, a light fluttered, shifted and died against the shadows. The bitterness increased. 'Oh, no. I might have known.'

'You might have known what?'

'I have three teenage brothers and sisters,' she said, sighing and lifting her purse from the seat in readiness to leave. 'They're all in the front room right now, and they're spying on us. I'll go in and they'll be all over me—they'll be so sympathetic about John and they'll be so avid for information about you...'

It'd drive him nuts. 'You don't ever think of moving out?'

'Oh, yeah.' She jeered gently into the night. 'Apartments are hardly thick on the ground in Bay Beach, and everyone would think we'd fought, and my mother would be hurt, and...' She glowered at the moving curtains, and then sighed. 'And I'd miss them.'

'I'm glad I don't have a family.'

That got to her. Her eyes widened in the dusk. No! 'Nick, you don't know what you're saying,' she whispered. She turned to him, shaken out of her self-pity, and she took both of his hands in hers in urgent entreaty. 'To not want a family... Nick, you just don't know...'

Then she took a deep breath, seemed to collect herself and she pulled away. She'd taken this too far. Exposed wounds she had no hope of healing. 'Th-Thank you for the ride home. Will I see you on Sunday?'

'I guess.' He smiled then, and softened. 'I'll be here. Shall I call for you at eleven and we'll collect Harry together?'

'He'll like that.'

And so will I, Nick thought suddenly. To leave her now with no future date in store would be hard. Shanni wasn't his sort, of course. Not as beautiful as the sophisticated women he normally dated. But...she was soft, warm, compassionate...

She was getting under his skin!

'You'd best go in,' he said uneasily, flicking a glance up at the shifting curtains. 'You'll be getting a reputation.'

'They've been watching me for ever,' she snapped. 'They drive me nuts. As if I'd ever do anything interesting...'

It was the way she said it. She didn't say it flatly—she

said it with longing. *As if I'd ever do anything interesting...*'

What did she want?

And suddenly he knew—or maybe it was what he wanted.

He laughed, a soft, carefree laugh that had her staring. 'Okay, then, Miss Uninteresting Miss McDonald...let's do something to give our audience a show. If you're willing...' His dark eyes dared her in the moonlight and then, before she knew or could guess what he intended, he took her into his arms and he kissed her.

CHAPTER SIX

THIS wasn't just a kiss.

This was a *kiss*!

It wasn't meant to be a kiss of friendship, a soft kiss of farewell, or even a kiss of the start of a love affair. This was passion meant for an audience. Nick had sized up three watching pairs of eyes and he knew what they most wanted—so he gave it to them in full.

His sports car was open to the weather and to their audience. The seats were wide and soft, and there was a good eighteen inches between driver and passenger. No more. Nick took a deep breath, turned to the lady beside him, put his hands on her shoulders—and kissed.

She leaned back with shock—and he leaned back with her, so they fell together onto the soft leather. She gave a squeak of astonishment. Their mouths met fleetingly as they disappeared underneath the dashboard—disappearing completely from view.

Then Nick lifted his face from hers momentarily—he'd had to stifle her squeak somehow, and kissing her properly was the only way to do it. 'Put your feet up high,' Nick whispered urgently before she could squeak again. 'A bit of stocking above the dash for the audience. Come on, Shanni, let's give them their money's worth.'

For a moment he didn't think she'd respond. Her body was rigid in his hold—shocked into immobility. Not for long, though. This was one smart lady, and her sense of humour was always bubbling just below the surface.

As somehow he'd known it would be, he thought. It was as if he knew her without knowing her, as if something in his mind read hers and understood. As he'd known it would—or he'd hoped.

And it happened. He felt laughter ripple though her body in a lovely long chuckle, and her arms came around him and held him fast. She leaped right into the act with a vengeance.

'Oh, Nick,' she murmured at full passion, her voice ringing out into the still, night air, carrying right up to the verandah and into the open window beyond. 'Nick... darling...'

'Shanni...' His mouth was inches from hers—once under the dash he could withdraw just a little. Laughter was bubbling inside him as well. 'A wiggle, I think,' he whispered urgently. 'A kick?'

And she did. With delight he felt her body shift under his. Her legs raised above dashboard height—she was wearing a flowing skirt, for heaven's sake, and her legs were silk-stockinged—and he felt her wiggle like crazy. Her feet waved back and forth like flags, as if she was riding a bicycle upside down. Inside the house, the siblings would be pop-eyed.

'Oh, Nick...' she groaned out loud. 'Nick, Nick...kiss me, kiss me...'

He choked with admiration and laughter, and he looked down into her laughing eyes.

And that was a mistake.

They were so lovely...

He was meant to be kissing the girl for a joke! She was laughing up at him, her stockinged feet were wiggling in the air and her eyes were alight with merriment. She was holding him, his body was pressed against hers and her breasts were moulding into his. Her laughing mouth was inches from his and she was so lovely...

And suddenly her mouth wasn't inches from his. It was right under his, and his mouth was on hers and he was kissing her—but he was kissing her as if there really was passion between them. As if this was a man making love to the most beautiful woman in the world—instead of an irrepressibly ridiculous small-town kindergarten teacher who wanted to tease her brothers and sister.

And Shanni had frozen again—but she froze only for one moment.

She could feel it too, he thought dazedly. Whatever was between them was shared, and it was something that was more powerful than either of them. This like-minded stuff…it was drawing them closer and closer, so her lovely laughing eyes merged with the twinkling of the stars and the feel of her body with his.

And night and girl and desire were all merging into one, and Nick was kissing her as if he'd never let her leave him—as long as they both should live.

'Shanni!'

It couldn't last, of course. How could it not end? Not with such an audience. The front door banged wide and a male voice shouted down to them from the verandah. 'Shanni, is that you?'

She didn't push away. Not instantly. For one tiny second they stayed together, and that fraction of an instant told Nick that Shanni was as reluctant to finish the kiss as he was.

But needs must. She pushed him back, and her eyes searched his in the dim light. And then she smiled, and if there was a trace of uncertainty in her smile it was replaced fast by laughter.

'Oh, Nick…what have you done? My reputation, forsooth…'

'What have *I* done? What have *you* done?' Somehow he managed laughter in return. 'Wicked Witch of the West and Scarlet Woman to boot.'

She grinned, hauling herself up to sit decorously again,

smoothing her skirt over her knees as both their heads reappeared above the dashboard for the observers to see.

'You're the seducer here,' she said primly. 'I can see the headlines now. ''Magistrate Seduces Innocent Kindergarten Teacher in Sports Car.'' You'll be tarred and feathered and run out of town.'

'I could be so lucky!'

She heard it then—the faint trace of bitterness in his voice. So he really did want to leave, she thought, and he wanted it badly. But...she couldn't focus on Nick any longer. Her father was out on the verandah, staring down at the couple in the car, and her mother was following close behind.

'Hi,' she managed, smiling up at her father. 'It's me, Dad. Nick gave me a ride home.'

'So I see.' The farmer's voice said he had a shotgun right behind him and he'd use it if necessary. To Nick's amazement, Shanni didn't blush or try to defend herself. She chuckled again and swung herself out of the car.

'Don't get your knickers in a twist, Dad. We had an audience.' She gestured to the curtain, where three faces had now appeared full-on. Her three youngest siblings. 'Nick thought we ought to give them a show for their money.'

'Oh...' Guy McDonald looked sideways at his three youngest children, worry fading as he saw what had happened. And he grinned. So this was where Shanni got her sense of humour. 'I see. So you shocked them to the core. Well done. You want to come in for coffee, young fella?'

'I...no. I need to get back.' Unlike Shanni, Nick wasn't in control at all. Something had happened during that kiss, and he wasn't at all sure he knew what it was. He needed to get back to town and sort out what he was feeling. Or...sort out that he was feeling *nothing*!

Which he must be.

'Nick's coming with us on Sunday, Dad,' Shanni said. She left the car, climbed the verandah steps, then stood between her parents and smiled back down at him. 'To Grandpa's birthday picnic. We're bringing Harry.'

'That's nice, dear,' her mother said placidly.

Did nothing shock these people?

No. It couldn't. Nick looked up at them. Guy McDonald's arm was around his daughter's shoulders, her mother was standing beside her with affection written clearly on her face, and the three young faces were still bobbing up and down at the window and grinning like three clowns—and Nick suddenly knew what it was he was seeing. This family loved their Shanni, and they loved her absolutely. Anything she chose to do would be okay by them.

The knowledge—the sensation—was suddenly almost claustrophobic. He'd never known a love like this. Never! And here she was, surrounded. Shanni was like an alien creature, he thought. She was totally apart from the world he lived in.

'I'll see you Sunday, then,' he said abruptly, and he flicked on the engine and spun the car around too fast in the driveway. A half-grown collie pup, heading down from the verandah to investigate, yelped and scurried for cover and Nick had to brake to avoid hitting him. Which sort of spoiled his dignified exit.

He made his exit anyway. He didn't look back—but Shanni and her parents stood on the verandah and watched him drive away, and he could feel their eyes follow him all the way into town.

'He's not your sort, is he dear?' Shanni's mother had no sooner closed the kitchen door and put the kettle on than she was into probe mode. Nick had been right. Anything

Shanni chose to do was okay with her parents, but that didn't mean they didn't enquire.

'It was a joke, Mum,' Shanni said mildly, and her mother flashed her a look that said she wasn't stupid.

'Your John's been telling the town you've thrown him over for the magistrate.'

'John's a chauvinist twit—and he's not *my* John.'

'He's a very worthy person,' her mother said sternly. Then a matching twinkle to her daughter's flashed into her older eyes. 'But you're right. He lacks a sense of humour, poor John. Your father and I are very relieved that you've finally seen it. It's only...'

'You think I'm jumping from the frying pan into the fire?'

'I would never have called John a frying pan.' Her mother chuckled and Shanni had to smile. 'But maybe...'

'Maybe nothing.' Shanni took a deep breath. 'I'm a big girl now, Mum, and I'm not looking to get involved with a magistrate. Especially one who's carrying the scars Nick is. But Harry thinks Nick is great and if I can get a relationship going between them... That baby needs someone who cares.'

'You care.'

'Harry needs a male.'

'He needs a daddy—and where there's a daddy there's usually a mother, too.'

'Oh, for heaven's sake...' Shanni glowered, half-laughing, half-indignant. 'Mum, I am *not* interested in Nick Daniels. Got it?'

'Yes, dear,' her mother said, and Shanni knew she didn't believe a word of it.

And maybe...maybe she didn't either.

And Nick?

Nick drove home feeling more claustrophobic than he'd

felt in his life before. All he wanted to do was to turn his car to head for the city and never come back.

Or was it? Wasn't it that he wanted to turn the car and return to Shanni?

No! He wanted to leave this town!

Which was really stupid. His career plans said he had to stick this place out for two years, and so far he'd done less than a week. Great! And he'd be welcomed back to the city with open arms—he didn't think!

If he appeared back in chambers next Monday morning they'd assume he'd failed. His long-term plan was high-court judge, and this was step one. He had to take it.

He didn't want to stay. He didn't want this involvement! Not with the child—or the girl.

He could concentrate on being a fine barrister, he thought desperately, and there was a possibility he could move sideways to the high court...

Ha! He'd looked at that option and he knew it depended hugely on luck. What he was doing now was the most certain way to get where he wanted. Put in the hard work, Abe had told him, and Abe was right.

Which meant putting up with country life—putting up with the gossip and the people—and staying uninvolved. But, for heaven's sake, he'd only been here for a few days and already he was involved up to his neck. He should ring Shanni and tell her their Sunday date was off.

'I do not want to go on a family picnic with a baby and a gorgeous girl and her grandma and grandpa and her brothers and sisters...'

Yes, he did. Sort of...

He wanted to be there, he knew, but he wanted to walk away at the end, heart-whole and fancy-free.

But he was starting to think there was no way that could happen, and the thought scared him witless.

* * *

Friday and Saturday were endless. Even the witnesses and defendants in court seemed to know what was happening in his life and to be summing him up.

'They think you're turning the place upside down,' Mary told him at the break of a long and boring case deciding whether a farmer's cows were damaging an access road. 'You arrive, we've had a hostage drama which will keep the district talking for years, the kindergarten teacher has broken off with her intended...'

'He wasn't her intended.'

'John sure intended, even if Shanni didn't. And now...the kids have spread it all over town that their sister's in love with you.'

They'd asked for that with their kissing stunt in the car, Nick thought wryly, and grimaced.

'I'm darned if I can see why everyone thinks it's their business.'

'This is Bay Beach,' Mary said simply. 'Everything's everyone's business. Speaking of which...'

'Don't...'

But she was unstoppable. 'I meant to tell you before this case started... Bill Nuggins could quite easily drive his cows to the dairy across his back paddock instead of using the road. He's using the road because the folk bought the place next door as a weekend home and he wanted to buy it himself. So now he likes the idea of them having to drive through cow dung.'

'Gee, thanks.' This was useful information but it wasn't up to his clerk of court to give it to him.

'Think nothing of it,' she said blandly. 'They're nice people and he's giving them a hard time so I thought you should know. I'm off after this, so I'll see you Sunday at the picnic. Oh, and you'd best make your mind up about Shanni. She's not one to tread water very long.'

What did she mean by that?

Nick didn't know, and he couldn't allow himself to care.

But he did care, and not just about Shanni. He finished work—advising the farmer to re-route his cows—took himself for a solitary walk on the beach and found his feet taking him to Harry's home. It was bedtime, and Wendy greeted him as if she'd been expecting him.

'He's been waiting for you.'

'I didn't say I'd come.'

'He knew you would.'

Nick figured he'd have to ignore that. Its implications were enormous. 'How did the assessment go today?'

'We're giving him another two weeks,' she said. 'If he doesn't settle by then...' She left the words unspoken but Nick knew exactly what she was saying. If Nick hadn't pulled off a miracle...

He shouldn't be here!

But, despite his reservations, he sat by the little boy's bed and read him a story about a *Very Dirty Dog* until Harry's eyes closed in weariness and he slipped into sleep. There was nothing else to do. And Harry needed him...

'He's so little and his body's still healing,' Wendy told him as he emerged, surprised by how ready for sleep Harry had been. 'He needs an afternoon sleep but he won't let himself relax. He's exhausted but he fights sleep every inch of the way.'

Why did that sound familiar? *If he closed his eyes, then things could happen. Bad things.* Nick remembered the sensation all too clearly. The world wasn't a safe place to sleep in...

'Shanni's taking him clothes-shopping tomorrow morning,' Wendy told him, closing the door on the sleeping child. She was carrying a little girl on her hip and there were two older boys making hot chocolate in the kitchen. Much as Wendy might care for Harry, there were limits to the personal attention he could get here, and Shanni must know it. 'She's picking him up at ten. Would you like to go with them?'

'No.' Nick shook his head. 'I'm busy.'

But the next day it took an iron will to keep him reading legal briefs in his apartment when he knew they'd be shopping. He had to read the briefs—if he didn't keep up with the legal world he'd turn into a country bumpkin—but Shanni and Harry were out choosing clothes without him and for some reason the thought was deeply disturbing.

This was crazy! He was going nuts.

One week down, he thought desperately. One hundred and three to go...

Beach day. Grandpa's birthday.

Nick woke at six and spent an hour composing urgent messages telling Shanni why he had to go to the city right now. Then he went for a jog on the beach, thought of a few more messages, showered, composed a few more...

Combed his hair flat. City-lawyer style.

Picked up the phone. Put down the phone.

Headed back to the shower, washed his hair again. Dressed. Combed his hair roughly and allowed his curls to dry any which way.

Went to collect Shanni.

'I was expecting you to cry off.'

'Were you?' He cast her a sideways glance. Shanni had been waiting on the verandah as he'd driven into the farmyard and she looked absolutely, breathtakingly lovely. She was simply dressed in a pink halter-neck top, the briefest of brief pink shorts and simple sandals. Her hair was sort of tousled and bunched on top. Her look was a million miles from that of any woman he'd dated in the city—and she looked a million dollars.

She wasn't his style. No!

'I was expecting myself to cry off,' he admitted. 'This isn't my scene.'

She grinned, teasing. 'Chicken.'

'I'd rather be a chicken than a dead hen.' He said it flippantly enough, staring at the road ahead, but she wasn't fooled for a minute. She looked at him for a long moment as he steered back onto the highway, and the smile she gave him became sympathetic.

'Hey, we're not that scary,' she said softly. 'Don't judges get to face murderers, gang lords and drug barons? What's a family picnic compared to that?'

What indeed? So there was no reason at all why his insides were telling him this was much, much scarier.

Harry was waiting, too, standing stolidly on the front porch with Wendy, with a look on his face that said he hadn't expected them to arrive at all. He didn't smile when he saw them, but the look of resignation lightened just a little, and when Wendy walked him to the car he didn't drag behind. He looked straight ahead, staring directly and unwaveringly at Nick—as if he was still expecting him to drive off fast.

Then he paused and looked at Nick's car—seeing it for the first time. The lightness faded, fear flooding back.

'I don't want to go...' he whispered.

'Harry doesn't like cars,' Wendy said, allowing him no time for protests but scooping him up and lifting him into Nick's minuscule back seat. 'But sometimes it's the only way to get where you want to go. Right Nick?'

'Right.' Nick turned and gave Harry a reassuring grin. There were two of them in this together, then. Two males who were both scared to death. And there was nothing for it but to go forward. Concentrate on something else but the fear...

'Hey, I like your shirt,' he told Harry, starting the engine and giving Shanni a sideways glance that begged for help.

He didn't need it. His comment was, apparently, exactly the right thing to say.

'Mmm.' Harry put his chin deep down on his chest and tried not to look pleased.

'We bought it yesterday,' Shanni told him. 'Harry and I went shopping for clothes, didn't we, Harry? It's a swimming T-shirt.'

'So I see.' The little boy's shirt had fish and sharks and octopuses all over it. Nick approved absolutely. 'It's a fine choice for today.'

'Your hair looks funny,' Harry said.

'Yeah.' It did too—and it felt funny. Nick put his fingers up and raked his curls self-consciously. He felt exposed like this. Weird.

'But it's a fine choice for today, too,' Shanni said solidly, and Nick looked across at her—and grinned. Maybe it didn't feel so bad after all.

'Nick's shirt's a bit boring, though,' she told Harry. 'Don't you think?'

'Hey…'

'I'm wearing pink spots and you're wearing fish,' she went on, confining her conversation to the child in the back. 'You'd think Nick could have found a shirt to wear that wasn't white.'

'It's short-sleeved,' Nick said, protesting. 'I'm not wearing a tie. It's fine.'

'It's white. Do magistrates have to wear white?'

'Yes. Always.' In truth, he owned nothing else.

'I'll bet they don't,' Shanni said thoughtfully. 'What do you reckon, Harry? I think Nick would look better in pink spots. Do you?'

Silence.

Then, to Nick's absolute astonishment, Harry chuckled.

At first he thought he'd imagined it. Shanni, too, looked

as if she'd been struck by lightning as the child's rich chuckle slowly formed and echoed around them.

They looked at each other. Nick and Shanni... Co-conspirators in lighting this child's life.

And then, slowly, Shanni's face broke into a smile that said all her Christmases had come at once—and then some.

'Pink,' she said, and if her voice was choked with emotion, then who could blame her. 'I'm buying our Nick a pink-spotted shirt first thing tomorrow morning, and no one in the whole world is going to stop me.'

And, after that, there was nothing to do but enjoy the day and accept that things were out of his control.

Shanni's extended family was enormous, with assorted cousins, aunts, nieces and nephews, boyfriends and hangers-on like himself, all equally welcomed into the chaos. There were kids and dogs and food and more food. There was beach cricket, swimming, sandcastles... Nick was drawn into the fray the minute he arrived.

He'd worn his swimming shorts under his clothes; his trousers and shirt were hauled from him by Rob the moment he arrived, half a gallon of sun lotion was slapped over him, Harry's cast was tied in an enormous plastic bag to keep it clean, and he and Harry were declared official cricket umpires.

'Magistrate work,' Rob decreed, and Shanni chuckled and disappeared toward the water.

'That's right. Make him useful.'

There was part of Nick that wanted to follow Shanni—but she didn't look back.

Then they were made sandcastle judges.

'Biggest is not best, either,' Shanni told him in passing as she headed to prepare the picnic. It was almost as if she was avoiding him.

And it kept happening.

After lunch Harry was scooped up and placed on a floating air-bed, the towrope was put in Nick's hand and he was sent out to sea with his passenger. And Shanni, again, was elsewhere. The family assumed Nick was here with Harry—not with Shanni. Nick found the sensation odd. Not bad but...odd.

He was accustomed to women taking notice of him—to women sticking as close as Harry—but Shanni wasn't sticking at all. To Shanni he seemed just one of the mob. She was taking Mary's kids out to sea on their own air-beds, she was swimming races, diving, surfacing for air, laughing with delight whether she won or lost, and then setting up the next race.

Then she swooped in and made her own sandcastle—when he and Harry were batting at cricket, with Nick guiding the little boy's hands.

Anything he was doing, she wasn't.

It finally started to rile him. By mid-afternoon he was sure it wasn't happening by accident. He could watch her all he wanted, but only from a distance. And she was so lovely...

'You'll have to move fast,' Mary said into his ear, and he jumped. He'd been a million miles away. Harry was settled on a towel by his side, three-quarters asleep and leaning heavily against him in sleepy contentment. They were sated with sun, sand and picnic, and Nick was finding it as hard as Harry to focus.

But while Harry was finding it hard to focus on anything, Nick was simply finding it hard to focus on anything that wasn't Shanni.

'I...what do you mean?' For some reason it was hard to get his voice working.

'Just what I said.' Mary plonked herself down on a towel and looked affectionately over at her sister. 'There's never much of a gap between Shanni's men.'

'I don't know what business...'

'There never is for any of the McDonald girls,' Mary said smugly, ignoring his interruption and looking across at her husband with affection. 'They're always snapped up, by the most gorgeous of men. My Mike included.'

'Mary...'

'Take me, for instance,' she said placidly. 'I was married at nineteen and I could have been married a whole heap earlier if I hadn't been very, very fussy.' She motioned across to where Louise and her young man were building a sandcastle together. 'I'm betting this little sister won't be far behind—she and Alastair can't keep their eyes off each other—and Hatty already has boyfriends even though she's only fifteen. It's only Shanni who's slow on the uptake, and that's because she can't choose.'

'I don't...'

'Eleven proposals,' Mary said sagely, shaking her head at the wonder of it. 'And that's just the serious ones. It's now starting all over again. Mum tells me, since the town found out John's a thing of the past, the phone's been running hot.'

'Your sister's very attractive,' Nick said stiffly, and Mary chuckled.

'She is and all.'

'I don't...' he started, but she shook her head.

'You do, so why not admit it?' she said, rising and shaking the sand from her towel. 'Ugh. I'm coated.' And then she fixed Nick with a stern look. 'But, whatever you do, do it fast. Because, as I said, there's a queue.'

She would not go near him.

Shanni was aware of the eyes of her family on her—what had started out as a joke had them all so interested it was almost sickening. They were agog—and she wasn't interested!

She wasn't!

If only Nick wasn't so...wasn't so...

Different.

And that difference was impossible to define. In so many ways he was the same as other men she'd gone out with. He had a great grin—yes, it was wonderful. But other men had great grins. He was strong—he must have swum since toddlerhood—his lean figure had towed Harry effortlessly on his floating mat and he'd won every race with her various male cousins. But...other men were strong.

And tender... He was amazingly tender. The way he had lifted Harry, the way he had put sun lotion on the little boy and wiggled patterns down the child's back, making him squeal in delight. The way he'd said something great about every kid's sandcastle...

Other men were great with kids.

It was more than that. It was the way he just was. The way he was just...Nick.

She saw so much that she knew he didn't want anyone to see: the way he looked at Harry, as if he couldn't believe he was committing himself, the way he looked around at her family, as if he was hungering for something he'd never had, and yet wanted so badly, the way he looked at her...

The way she seemed to know what was right there in his heart.

It scared her rigid. And...all her family were watching.

She wasn't interested. She *wasn't*!

She avoided him like the plague.

It was almost dusk as they drove home. They'd eaten tea on the beach—Shanni's grandpa had ordered pizzas, and one of the enduring images Nick would take home from this day was the pizza delivery boy hiking over sand-hills with a dozen or more boxes balanced precariously before him.

Then Shanni's mum had produced a birthday cake, grandpa had blown out seventy candles, the birthday song had been bellowed by the entire family and the day had been declared officially over.

And it had left Nick feeling…empty? As if he'd been allowed to glimpse something that could never be his.

He'd half expected to go home alone with Harry, but as he'd put the little boy into the car—he was already fast asleep—Shanni had emerged from the crowd of her family and tossed her bag in beside him.

He was therefore deemed her chauffeur. According to Mary, he should feel honoured.

He didn't. He just felt…more empty. As if he was being allowed more insight into what could never be his.

'Cat got your tongue?' She smiled at him as he started the engine. Her hair was escaping every which way from her crazy topknot, she was sand-coated, her nose was pink-tipped from too much sun—and he had an almost overwhelming urge to stop the car and kiss her.

He did no such thing. The emptiness was almost tangible. But emptiness was his life. It was what he was accustomed to, and he didn't know how the heck to cope with anything else.

So he steered the car toward the town and he clenched his hands on the steering wheel and he said nothing.

For a few minutes she watched him in matching silence. 'Nick, what's wrong?' she asked at last, and the teasing tone had become serious.

'Nothing.'

'When I say that to my kindergarten students and they say, "nothing," it usually means they've just made a puddle.'

He grinned at that. 'Miss McDonald, I can assure you that I haven't made a puddle.'

'I'm very glad to hear it.' She looked at him for a long

moment, questioning, and then gave a slight shrug and
turned to look over her shoulder at the sleeping Harry.
'He's had a wonderful day,' she said softly.

'Yes,'

'And you, Nick? You've had a good time?'

'I…yes.'

'I'm glad,' she said warmly, probing no deeper. 'My
family think you're great.'

'Because I'm not John?'

'There is that.' She chuckled. 'Oh, dear. I was a twit for
thinking I could marry him.'

'There'll be other fish in the sea.'

'I guess…' Her voice faded. 'Nick…'

'Mmm?'

She looked across at him as if she was about to ask
something, thought better of it and pressed her lips together.
More silence. Then the town boundary came into view, and
it was say something now or the opportunity would be over.

'Will you see Harry again?' she asked.

'I don't know,' he said stiffly. 'Not for a while.'

'Because you're busy,' she agreed cordially. 'I guess.'

'I need to go to Melbourne next weekend.'

'To change suits and ties? I hoped you'd kicked the
habit.'

He grinned at that. 'Yes, okay. I've kicked the habit. But
I do have another life.'

'You have a girlfriend in town?'

'No.'

'I see.' She didn't see at all. She stared ahead as the car
turned into the street leading to the children's home. Time
was running out. It was now or never…

'Nick, Harry's dad took him to Melbourne every weekend,' she said, her voice suddenly urgent. 'He worked here
in the timber mill, but every Friday night he and Harry
headed for the city. Harry's grandmother lived there.'

'He has a grandmother?'

'She died just before Peter did. But Harry still remembers going to the city.'

'Are you suggesting,' Nick said slowly, thinking this through, 'that I take Harry to Melbourne?'

'I don't see why not. I think he'd love it.'

'I can't cope with a baby on my own.'

She thought about that and shook her head. 'Of course you can.' She was all decisive now, right back into the bossy mode Nick was starting to know and, he had to admit, enjoy. 'You're a clever, competent man, Nick Daniels, and Harry is one very small boy. You can cope if you want.'

'Then I don't want,' he said bluntly. Harry in his favourite restaurants or with his sophisticated friends? No and no and no.

But now Shanni was looking at him as if he'd personally betrayed her.

He couldn't let it matter, he told himself desperately. He couldn't let her drag him into this mess so that he was personally involved.

But yet... As he stopped the car and went to lift the sleeping Harry from the back seat, he was aware of a lurch of pain in his gut.

Harry was so small. His cast looked so heavy and there were shadows of tiredness on his pale little face. He stirred in sleep, his eyes fluttered open and he smiled, just ever so faintly, as he saw who was carrying him. Then his eyes fell closed again and he relaxed absolutely in Nick's arms.

Nick might not want to get personally involved—but he was already.

He had to walk away.

*   *   *

And with Harry safely left in Wendy's charge—the little boy hadn't stirred as they washed him and popped him into bed—he had to take Shanni home. Another five minutes in the car. Get this over with fast, he told himself harshly. Move on.

But as the car pulled into the farmyard he was aware of a stab of absolute longing—to somehow prolong the moment.

'I...they tell me it's the mayoral ball on Friday week,' he told her, and he was speaking too fast. Which confused him totally. For heaven's sake, he didn't mess up invitations. Where was the smooth Nick Daniels now? 'I gather I'm expected to attend. I don't suppose you'd like to go with me?'

She stared at him for a long minute, considering.

'Isn't that a bit dangerous?' she said at last, her teasing voice back. 'You'd be expected to dance with me.'

'Dancing's okay.'

'Just not emotion.'

'I guess.'

She sighed and shook her head, teasing fading. 'Nope. This is never going to work. You won't even let a tiny little boy touch your life.'

'Hey, I'm not asking for emotional entanglement here,' he said, startled. 'Just a date.'

'I know you're not asking for emotional entanglement.' She sounded angry, and he stared.

'What's wrong? You're upset that I won't take Harry to Melbourne next weekend?'

She tilted her chin. 'Yes,' she said flatly. 'I am. You have the chance to do so much good, Nick Daniels, and you daren't do it because of your precious independence. You won't take a risk—and Harry suffers because of it.'

'So if I said I'd take Harry to Melbourne then you'd come to the ball with me?'

It was the wrong thing to say and he knew it the moment the words were uttered. She drew in her breath in a sharp, angry hiss and she drew away from him, her anger tangible in the still night air.

She was struggling for words—struggling to say anything. And, in the end, all she could manage was a furious, 'How dare you?'

His brows rose. What on earth was she on about? 'How dare I what?'

She was almost beside herself with anger. 'You'd barter a little boy's love for…a *date*?'

'That's not what I said.'

'That's exactly what you said,' she snapped. She hauled herself out of the car, slammed the door shut and glared at him for all she was worth. The emotions of the day bubbled to boiling point, and the steam had to be let out somehow. And here it came!

'You arrogant, selfish…toad!' she threw at him. 'You know what Harry needs. He needs a friend who cares for him. That's all. He's not asking anything more of you than that. But you sit there in your icy, calculating world and you won't let anyone near. And everything's bought or sold or thought of as payment due. Take Harry to Melbourne and get yourself a date for a ball you don't want to go to. Come and be a country magistrate and get yourself the next step up the career ladder. Buy and sell—and don't ever get involved. You make me sick, Nick Daniels. You make me absolutely sick.'

'Shanni…'

'Goodbye.'

And she stalked up the verandah steps without saying another word, while Nick sat stunned.

The front door slammed shut behind her.

And Nick wasn't able to see that, with the door safely closed, Shanni leaned against it and burst into tears.

CHAPTER SEVEN

'MESSED up your love life, have you?'

'I beg your pardon?' Gowned and groomed—if you didn't count his non-smoothed hair—Nick was ready for his Monday morning list. So was Mary.

'You're glowering like you've just learned you're having no holidays for a year—and our Shanni's looking the same.'

'What Shanni does is nothing to do with me.'

'Funny.' Mary tossed him an impudent grin. 'That's what Shanni says about you. We'll just have to see what happens.'

'Mary...'

'Hmm?'

'Put a sock in it,' he said dourly. And then he stared at his court list. 'Mary, why does it say Bart Commin is appearing first up? I thought I sentenced him to ten days...'

'We're appealing,' she said cheerfully. 'Rob organised it. Emma's going nuts.'

'How can it be an appeal when he's not being represented?'

'Rob's representing him.'

'A policeman,' Nick said carefully, 'cannot lodge an appeal.'

'Where does it say that?' Mary demanded, and Nick stared.

'I...'

'They often do,' she told him kindly—clerk of courts dispensing wise legal advice to magistrate. 'Surely you know that. The state has the right to appeal if they believe

118

the sentence is too lenient. So we figured, what if the sentence is too tough? What's the difference?'

'Mary...'

'Which it is,' she told him sternly. 'Bart's screaming the place down. Shivering, sobbing—the works. If you let him out then old Doc Harris will pop him in hospital for a couple of days; he'll sort him out and we'll all be happy.'

'I'll organise him to be shifted to hospital while he serves his time.'

'Not here you can't, Your Worship,' she said primly. 'Not while he's supposed to be in jail. Bay Beach has a country bush hospital with no secure wards. He'd have to go to the Warrbook hospital, and he'd hate it.'

'Oh, great. So now we're into personal preferences.' Nick raked his hair in exasperation. 'Mary, he's a prisoner. He's a convicted thief with a record longer than your arm.'

'He's stolen nothing but beans—and he's a nice old man.' Mary's voice was reproachful. 'He might be a drunk but we all like him. Go on, Nick. Have a heart.'

So fifteen minutes later Nick found himself reducing Bart's sentence by six days—and he found himself wondering just how much more heart was required in this job. And how much more he had to give.

Harry required heart.

All day Monday Harry stayed in his mind, niggling like a bad conscience. And all day Tuesday.

Shanni was in his mind too—but there was nothing he could do about Shanni, he told himself savagely. Shanni didn't need him.

And he couldn't even begin to think that he might need her.

No. Concentrate on Harry. Leave Shanni to her queues of suitors... He *had* to concentrate on Harry.

Tuesday night he walked over to the home and almost

knocked on the door—and then he walked away. He did a few miles of jogging on the beach, came back, stared at the darkened children's home, swore at himself and then went back to his apartment above the courthouse. And thought...

Shanni. Harry. Shanni....

Harry! Wednesday night he returned, and this time he knocked. It was too hard not to.

'Nick.' Wendy met him at the door, her face wary. There were two little girls in the hall, playing with dolls. Wendy half opened the door but she didn't invite him in. 'Can I help you?'

'I came to see Harry.'

'Have you, now?' There was caution in her voice—not the open friendliness she'd shown him last week.

What had Shanni said to her?

But Shanni, it seemed, hadn't said a word. The wariness was all Wendy's.

'Harry had a lovely day on Sunday, Nick,' she said. 'Just wonderful. But then...on Monday he sort of thought you'd come. Shanni didn't know if you would, I wasn't sure, so I rang the courthouse. Mary said she'd have you ring back. Didn't you get my message?'

Yeah. He'd got the message. It had taken him up until now to figure out what he wanted to say.

'I'm sorry.'

'Harry doesn't mind you not coming so much,' Wendy said. 'Well, to be honest, he does mind, but he can cope. What he can't cope with is not knowing where he stands with you. Whether he has a friend or not.'

And there it was. If he committed now he'd be committing totally. This wasn't like a relationship with an adult that he could explain away at some time in the future.

Not like his relationship with Shanni...

For heaven's sake. Think of Harry. Harry! There was no way he could back out now.

'Can I talk to you?' he said.

'I'm here to be talked to,' Wendy said. She held the door open a little wider but still she didn't invite him in. 'Harry's in the kitchen. Talk here.'

You need to make a decision before you go one step further, her voice warned him, and he nodded.

'Wendy, I'm not talking about taking Harry on long-term or anything,' he warned. 'I can't adopt him or foster him.'

'No one's asking you to do that.' Her eyes were still wary, and she was reading his eyes. 'Harry isn't asking that. He expects nothing of the world. But he needs a friend. Desperately. A friend who's constant—who says I'll see you once a week and who doesn't break that promise unless there's a darned good reason and Harry knows what that reason is.'

'Once a week…'

'Any less than that and it's not worth it,' she said bluntly. 'He's just a baby, and he's too little to remember. So, yes. Once a week or nothing.'

Nick took a deep breath.

And took the plunge.

'I can do that.'

There. It was said. The commitment made him take a step back. He'd never made such a promise in his life. But…it wasn't such a bad feeling.

Except it scared him half to death. And Wendy saw.

'Did you ever have any decent relationships with anyone?' she asked gently. 'When you were little?'

'I…no.'

She shook her head, and the wariness was gone. There was only gentleness and caring left. 'Then, praise be,' she said softly, 'it seems Bay Beach has itself quite a magistrate. If you can get over that…'

'Hey, I don't...'

'You already have,' she said warmly, and threw the door wide. 'Tonight you've taken the first step. Let's see where we go from here.'

He still had to go to Melbourne for the weekend. It wasn't just ties, he thought dryly. He'd only brought necessities, thinking he'd be back and forth all the time, so he needed to go.

But when he told Wendy and Harry that...

'I like Melbourne,' Harry said, sitting up at the kitchen table eating a bowl of chocolate ice cream and trying not to look as if he'd been given the world because *his* Nick had come to visit. Because *his* Nick was eating chocolate ice cream beside him. 'Me and Daddy went to Melbourne every weekend.'

'Did you?' It was impossible for Nick not to hear the hint in the little boy's voice. The longing...

And for a whole five seconds he stayed strong. But Wendy was watching him. Daring him. Wendy who was Shanni's friend, and Nick knew what Shanni would expect him to do.

Harry was watching, too, with eyes that said he expected nothing.

It was too much. A tougher man than him would break under this pressure.

'Would you like to come?'

'Yes,' Harry said, so promptly that Nick nearly choked on his ice cream. For heaven's sake, what had he done?

But it was too late to draw back now.

'I'll pick you up on Friday after work,' he said, casting a desperate look at Wendy. She grinned.

'See—doesn't hurt at all.'

'I don't know how to care for him—look after his leg...'

'I'll write you a list of instructions,' she said blithely.

'But kid-care's a doddle. Easy as falling off a log. I'll even organise a booster seat for the car.'

But there was one more problem and it wasn't Nick's. 'I…I don't want to go in the car,' Harry said, and his voice was suddenly desperately anxious. He even stopped ice-cream-eating. Wendy sighed, scooped him up and placed him on her knee. She understood this fear.

'Harry, you and your daddy had a terrible car crash but that was a really unlucky time. It's not going to happen again.'

But Harry was torn. Nick could see it. He desperately wanted to go to Melbourne—with his Nick—but hours in a car with all of his dreadful memories was almost too much to face.

Okay, then. In for a penny… 'We'll take the train,' Nick said.

Wendy almost dropped Harry. 'You're joking.'

'I never joke,' Nick said heavily. 'More's the pity. We'll catch the evening train on Friday. Will you be ready, Harry?'

'Yes,' he said joyfully, and he wriggled off Wendy's lap and burrowed his face into his ice cream as if it was champagne.

What had he done?

He couldn't believe he'd offered. For the next couple of days Nick worked in a stunned stupor. Taking a tiny child to Melbourne… Giving up his car for the weekend…

His friends would die laughing.

They wouldn't see, he decided. He couldn't take Harry to his usual haunts.

Where would he take him?

'You're quiet,' Mary said, as she gave him his Friday court list. Heaven knew whether she'd heard of his weekend plans. Probably not, he decided. She'd have said something. But it was unlike this town to keep things quiet. For Wendy not to talk...

Mary was waiting for an answer and he had to dredge one from somewhere. 'It's just...I'm looking forward to a weekend away.'

'I'll bet you are,' she said softly, and her eyes held a look he didn't understand in the least.

He was running late. Since when did court cases ever run to time? he thought bitterly, grabbing his overnight bag and heading for the station with speed. He had minutes before the train left. Please let Wendy have Harry on the platform.

She did, and she had tickets in her hand as well. Bless her. The whistle blew as she handed over tickets, Harry's overnight bag—and Harry.

'Have fun, boys,' she called as they disappeared into their carriage. And then she grinned.

'And have fun, Shanni,' she added, and she walked away with her fingers crossed.

Car three, compartment five...

The train jolted into motion; Harry clung onto Nick's hand like grim death and they made their way carefully down the corridor as Nick checked seat allocation.

'I wonder if we have the compartment to ourselves,' Nick said, and then he stopped.

He was at the right door, but there was already a passenger in the compartment.

It was Shanni.

For all of ten seconds they stared at each other, shocked into immobility. In the end it was Harry who broke the silence. His smile, unused for so long, now threatened to split his face.

'Are you coming to Melbourne with us?' he asked her, deeply pleased.

'I am, but...' Nick saw she was as flabbergasted as he was. 'Are you going on the train to Melbourne, too?'

'Yes,' said Harry firmly, hitching himself up on to the seat beside Shanni and wriggling his small backside deep into the leather. 'I am. Me and Nick.'

'Why,' she asked carefully, looking at Harry and not at Nick, 'are you not driving to Melbourne in Nick's car?'

'I don't like cars,' Harry said.

Silence while she chewed that one over. Nick put the baggage up in the racks and tried to think of something to say. Anything.

She was as stuck for words as he was, and when she finally spoke her voice was loaded with bitterness. 'I think,' Shanni said carefully, 'that I've been set up.'

'Not by me,' he told her, and sat down opposite. Nick's voice sounded angry, and Harry looked at him in surprise. Unnoticed, the train gathered speed and Bay Beach faded into the distance behind them.

'I guess I could always get off at the next stop.' Shanni looked as if she'd like to jump off right now.

Great. But... Nick bit his lip and looked at Harry's drooping face. He'd looked so pleased! 'Why are you going to Melbourne?' he enquired at last.

'To visit my Aunt Adele. She's ill, and my mother's worried.'

'I see.'

'Except now...' She was deep in thought, not seeing him, and she was almost talking to herself. 'My family have been odd. Mary's been telling me how worried Mum was about Adele, and Mum was sort of agreeing—only not saying much—and then when I said I'd phone Adele, Rob said Emma phoned her this morning and she was miserable. Then Mary offered to buy me a train ticket. As the family contribution...'

'You think they've set this up?' Nick said. He couldn't

see any other reason behind this, and he wouldn't put it past Mary for a minute.

'I wouldn't be the least bit surprised.' Shanni's anger matched his. 'John came around last night and Louise told him—right in my hearing—that he wasn't welcome and I was in love with *you*! He drove off before I could reach him. I ask you. In love with…*you*!'

She said *you* as if he was some sort of dung-beetle— and, despite his annoyance, Nick had to grin.

'Which is ridiculous,' he said politely.

'Which is ridiculous,' she said, and glowered.

'So what do we do?'

'We're all going to Melbourne,' Harry said, pleased again now Shanni had stopped talking of getting off. 'You and me and Nick.'

'I imagine we can put up with each other for the journey,' Nick said politely. 'You never know, your aunt might be sick.

'She might not be.' Shanni sighed, anger giving way to exasperation. 'I guess I can shop.'

'Will you shop with me?' Harry asked anxiously, and Shanni managed a smile.

'Hey, you and I shopped last Saturday. You haven't worn those clothes out yet?'

'No, but…'

'You and Nick are having a boys' weekend,' she told him. 'You don't need a lady.'

'You're not a lady,' he told her. 'You're you.'

'*That* sounds the very nicest thing anyone has ever said about me,' she told him, still smiling. 'But flattery will get you nowhere, Harry, my lad. It's a boys' weekend and I don't need anything to do with it.'

Which meant, as the train arrived at Melbourne, Harry and Nick prepared to bid Shanni farewell. Or Nick prepared to. Harry had other ideas.

'Where does your aunty live?' Harry demanded.

'Brighton.'

'Is that close to where we're going?' This was one bright kid—and he was certainly persistent.

Nick nodded reluctantly. 'Yes. We're going to St Kilda, which is on the way to Brighton.' Then, because it was the only polite thing to say, he added a rider. 'Would you like to share a cab?'

'That would be nice,' Shanni said, smiling at Harry but eyeing Nick with reservations. 'And then separate directions. Right?'

'Right.'

Only, once in the cab, Harry started to talk. He'd been his usual silent self on the train journey, but now he seemed to sense there was some urgency about proceedings.

'What will you and your aunty do for the weekend?' he asked Shanni.

'If my aunty's sick then I'll look after her. What are you boys going to do?'

Nick shrugged. 'I'm not sure. We'll think of something.'

'Will you meet us for just a little bit?' Harry said, and suddenly there was the faintest tremor in his voice. He looked uncertainly at Nick, and his look said he'd suddenly remembered he didn't know this man very well. For all he knew, Nick could be planning a weekend doing very boring grown-up things—and Miss McDonald was fun.

'I...' Shanni wasn't sure what her response should be. She'd heard the tremor.

'Come shopping with us,' Harry urged.

She glanced at Nick—and then glanced away again. 'I may not be able to.'

And Nick sighed. He knew when he was being bulldozed, and he was being bulldozed now. It would make

Harry feel more secure if he knew he'd see Shanni again, so there was no choice.

'I'll take Harry to one of the cake shops in Acland Street tomorrow morning,' he said grudgingly. 'Join us for coffee. If your aunt can spare you…'

'Or if I can spare my aunt,' she said—and looked at Harry. 'Okay, Harry. I make no promises, but you just might see me tomorrow morning.'

There was no time for more. The taxi pulled up outside the address Nick had given, and she gazed up in stunned silence. Nick's apartment was in a three storeyed block right on the esplanade overlooking the ocean. She didn't need to see any closer to figure this place had cost him a mint.

No wonder he hadn't been too impressed with his sea view at Bay Beach. He had his own sea view here, surrounded by city comforts.

'Wow!' said Harry.

'Double wow,' said Shanni. St Kilda was only ten minutes from the city and her aunt's place at Brighton was further out. It had made sense, therefore, for the taxi to drop Nick and Harry off first. So now she knew where he lived—and his obvious wealth didn't make getting to know the man any easier. They had even less in common than she'd thought.

He was a lawyer and a magistrate and he was wealthy. He was a man alone…. A man completely out of her ken. She watched in silence as Nick handed payment to the taxi driver—and then frowned as he demurred at the change.

'No. The lady's fare is on me.'

'Nick, you don't need to…' she started, but he allowed no protest.

'It'll make me feel better to make sure you're safely home.'

Or…safely away from you, Shanni thought bleakly as

the taxi did a U-turn and drove away from man and child. Leaving you to your precious independence.

But...why on earth did the thought make her feel so bleak?

It wasn't only Shanni who was questioning feelings. Nick might have his independence—sort of—but independence wasn't something that sat well with three-year-olds.

He showed Harry into the spare room. Harry looked at the enormous bed and his eyes stayed blank in a look Nick was starting to know. It was his withdrawal look.

'It's a great big bed,' Nick said cheerfully. He'd fitted his spare room with a double bed because most of his friends were partnered—spasmodically. 'You can sleep in the middle and wiggle all you want.

'Where do you sleep?' Harry asked in a subdued little voice that told Nick he was in even more trouble than he'd thought.

'Next door. Want to see?'

He did, so Nick led the way, opened the bedroom door and heard Harry gasp.

'Do you sleep in that bed all by yourself?'

'Yep.' Well, most of the time, anyway, and he wasn't going into that with a three-year-old.

'It's...it's *ginormous*.'

'It is.' Nick smiled and led the little boy forward. 'It's called a king-sized bed. Actually,' he admitted, 'it's two beds. It's so big I couldn't get it up the stairs in one piece, so I brought two single beds and joined them together. See?' He lifted the covers, Harry dropped down on the plush pile carpet and inspected eight legs.

'It *is* two beds,' he agreed. 'Why do you sleep in two beds?'

'I...I like room to wiggle.'

'If we pulled them apart then we could have a little bed

each in the same room,' Harry said wistfully—and waited. His eyes were still blank—as if he was afraid to hope.

That hadn't been in the plan. Sleep in the same room as Harry!

But Harry was looking at him with dreadful eyes—eyes that told him the thought of sleeping in a huge bed in a bedroom all by himself held nothing but terror. Oh, great... Big choice here!

So... 'I guess we can,' Nick agreed faintly, and watched the blank look fade.

'You'd like that,' Harry told him, and his eyes dared Nick to agree. 'We could talk in bed.'

'So we could.' He hadn't thought of that, either.

'Wendy says I have to go to bed at eight o'clock. Do you go to bed at eight o'clock?'

There was nothing for it. Nick nodded with all due solemnity. 'Not usually,' he said truthfully. 'But this weekend I just might.'

He did. In the end it was easier, because Harry couldn't settle. He lay and stared at the ceiling while Nick read him a story, and when Nick finished reading his eyes were just as firmly open as when he'd started. When Nick tried to leave the room he said nothing—just stayed staring up at the ceiling with a fixed expression of stoicism.

He'd been here before, the expression said. Strange place. Strange people. Strange shadows.

Familiar fear...

And Nick, who remembered the feeling as if it were yesterday, couldn't bear it.

'I *am* tired,' he told Harry. 'I think I'll come to bed, too.'

'That'd be okay,' Harry said, still stoical. He was so careful not to let his eagerness show, in case this wonderful offer should be snatched away again.

So Nick slid between the covers of his now single bed

and stared at the ceiling himself in the half-light—for heaven's sake, at eight it was hardly dark.

And, while Harry drifted firmly into sleep, Nick wondered what Shanni was doing.

And wondered and wondered and wondered.

CHAPTER EIGHT

COFFEE and cakes in Acland Street was an institution. The street had been the cake centre of Melbourne for generations, each shop vying to supply the most mouth-watering cakes and each shopfront more wonderful than the last.

Nick and Harry wandered hand in hand for half an hour as Harry checked every cake. Nick was content to do as Harry wished. Two weeks ago cake-choosing would have bored him silly, but he'd come a long way in two weeks. To give Harry pleasure was pleasure enough, and his mind had things to dwell on.

Finally Harry made his choice—sponge cake topped with meringue, strawberries and chocolate. And he wanted a rather strange-sounding lemonade and lime drink too—a lime spider! Nick gave his approval—this place had great coffee too—and they settled on a table outside on the pavement like long-term friends,

'I like this place,' Harry said in a very muffled voice. His mouth was full of cake. He took a sip of his lime spider and thought about it, then paused and his face clouded. 'I don't think my daddy brought me here.' He stared down at his cake and his voice fell away. 'I can't even remember if he liked cakes.'

'He loved cakes.'

And here she was! Nick spun around to see Shanni bearing down from behind. She was dressed in a lovely light linen dress, her hair was flying free and she was laden with shopping—she must have a dozen carrier bags!

'Hi, boys.' She beamed her pleasure at finding them, dumped her bags in a huge pile and plonked herself onto a spare seat. 'Phew. Harry, your daddy was the biggest cake-eater in Bay Beach. When the local school had its fête he was first in the queue for the cake stall, and, by the look of that cake you take right after him. What a great choice. Can I have one, too?'

She kicked off her sandals, sighed with relief and beamed again at the pair of them. 'Aren't I clever to find you? We didn't even make a definite time or a place.'

'Very clever,' Nick said dryly—there was no hint in his voice of the lurch of pleasure he'd felt at the sight of her—and Shanni's beam broadened.

'You might at least sound pleased to see me. Harry, are you pleased to see me?'

'Yes,' Harry said definitely. 'I am. Nick's bed's too big. We had to chop it in half.'

'I see.' Her perplexed forehead said she didn't see at all but she was game to try. 'So…tell me all. You chopped Nick's bed in half. With an axe?'

'No, silly.' Harry giggled and Shanni's eyes met Nick's. There was a message clearly written—congratulations! Her smile was almost patronising, Nick thought, but he felt his chest expand a notch. His world had lightened just a little.

Or maybe a lot. He hadn't wanted to see her—but now she was here…

'Shanni, we think we might be bored now,' Harry was confiding. 'After our cake we don't know what to do. Nick says we might visit a lawyer he knows who has a baby.'

'Do you want to do that?' Shanni asked.

Harry buried his nose in lime spider. 'No,' he whispered, avoiding Nick's eyes.

Shanni smiled again. Goodness! A Harry ready to assert himself. This was something indeed. 'I see.' Her eyes flew to Nick's, gently mocking. 'Time for a rethink, then, Your Worship.'

'I'll figure it out.' He signalled for more coffee—he

needed it!—and cake and spider for Shanni, and when he turned back Harry and Shanni were deep in her parcels. Harry was peering into one parcel after the other, his whole head disappearing.

'They're all clothes,' he said, emerging disgusted, and Nick grinned.

'Women do that.'

'Yeah, and men buy hair cream and silk ties. Bought your semi-trailer-load yet?' Shanni's eyes flew to his unruly mop and he grinned self-consciously.

'Well, no.' This felt strange, he thought. Weird. But…good. To be sitting in the sun with a funny, bubbly lady and a kid who no one wanted but who looked at him as if he knew everything. As if he liked him…

It wasn't a sensation Nick had ever experienced, and he wasn't quite sure what to do with it.

Go with the flow, he thought. And try to keep the goofy grin off your face…

'How's your aunt?' he asked, and Shanni wrinkled her pert nose in disgust.

'She isn't.'

That startled him. 'You mean…she's dead?'

'She's in Adelaide visiting an ancient schoolfriend,' Shanni said bitterly. 'She left last week. Ill, my foot! Lying, conniving family. You wait until I get my hands on them.'

'I…see.' He didn't quite. 'So you stayed in an empty house last night?'

'I stayed in a hotel.' She gave a beleaguered smile. 'My aunt's locked the place like Fort Knox, there are signs saying the house is guarded by the Automatic Shotgun, Doberman and Machete-Carrying Security Company, and I don't have a key. So I got to stay in a seedy, third-rate hotel…'

'Shanni, you can stay at Nick's,' Harry said urgently. The conversation was confusing but he had one point clear.

Shanni needed a bed—and he needed Shanni. The course, therefore, was crystal-clear. 'Nick has a whole bedroom he doesn't use and he has the biggest bed! Nick and me sleep in the chopped-up bed in Nick's room, so you can have the big bed.'

'Hey…' She was taken aback—and even more so when she glanced at Nick and found him smiling at her. Well, what else could he do?

'Yes, Shanni, it's free.' For heaven's sake, what was he saying? It was as if his mouth was forming words without his head being engaged, but he couldn't stop himself. 'Or…' He just had a brilliant thought! 'You could have the chopped-up bed if you like—with Harry—and I'll have the big one.'

'No,' Harry said urgently. 'You and me have to sleep in the chopped-up beds, Nick. Wendy says boys don't sleep with girls.'

Neither they do, Nick thought resignedly, watching Shanni grin and seeing every last vestige of a controlled weekend disappear before his eyes. Neither they do.

After elevenses Shanni went straight into bossy mode and they went rollerblading.

'Because you guys haven't decided what to do, it's up to me to organise something. I haven't been to the esplanade for years, but I bet they still rollerblade just like they did when I was here on teacher-training.'

'Can I go rollerblading?' Harry said, and Shanni nodded.

'Well, sort of. It'll be rollerpushing for you, my boy, until you get that leg straight, but I'll bet you'll enjoy it. Won't he, Nick?'

'Sure.' For the life of him, it was all he could think of to say. There was nothing for it but to agree.

So they dumped her gear in Nick's apartment—'*Great jumping Jehosophat!*' Shanni said when she saw Nick's expensive white and chrome decor, and Harry chortled his agreement—and headed down to hire equipment.

'I can't rollerblade in my leg cast,' Harry said sadly, seeing the equipment on offer and looking down at his ungainly leg. 'And I don't know how. Do I have to watch?'

He most certainly didn't.

'No,' Shanni decreed. 'I told you. It's rollerpushing for you. These are just the ticket.' And she motioned to the pushchairs beside the hire store.

'You're the navigator,' Shanni told him, belting him into a pushchair. Unlike normal strollers, this one had huge wheels and a high handle, built for parents who wanted to push children with speed. 'You say fast, and we'll go fast. You say stop then we stop.' She rethought that, and grinned up at Nick, who was too stunned to say anything. 'Or...we might stop. If we can. It's a long time since I wore rollerblades, and I don't know how good Nick is.'

'I'm good,' Nick said, affronted, and Shanni grinned.

'There you go, then. Your Nick's a lawyer, a magistrate and a rollerblade expert as well, Harry. What a man!'

And Nick knew she was mocking him but he was so far out of his depth that he couldn't care less. This was a day for putting pride aside.

For putting everything aside except the moment.

They rollerbladed for the day. With Harry before them they took a handle each and went flying along the beachfront—whizzing in and out of pedestrians and cyclists and dog-walkers as if they'd been born on wheels.

'Slow down,' Nick said at first, but Shanni grinned and increased speed.

'Wuss!'

And after that they didn't speak. Nick was totally befuddled—and there was no need to talk, anyway. The path was hardly crowded—it went for ever all the way along the beachfront toward the city—and their speed matched exactly.

Their movements matched exactly. When Shanni slowed, Nick slowed with her, anticipating every movement. When she turned, he turned. When a dog lunged toward them off its lead they braked as one, waited until the dog shot across their path and then scooted on again, Harry squealing with delight.

Nick watched her out of the corner of his eyes. Her curls were flying, her eyes were dancing, she looked alive and vibrant and free.

And gorgeous!

And Harry... The little boy was lit up like a Christmas tree. He sat bolt upright in his chair, his eyes were wide with excitement and he crowed with joy. Every now and then he looked up and grinned, and Nick and Shanni grinned back down at him—and then grinned at each other as he returned to the serious business of navigation.

Which seemed to be a simple matter of crowing, 'Faster, faster, faster,' until Shanni flung back her head, her curls flying and she choked on a bubble of laughter and slowed...

'Here, slave-driver. What did your last horse die of? I'm about to leave my legs behind me at this speed... Nick, okay, I concede, I concede. Slow down!'

They slowed—but not much. They left the beach and followed the bike-path until they reached the river, then slowed as the crowds thickened on the river-banks, but still they wove dexterously through. Still there were no words spoken. They knew what the other intended. It was like a sixth sense.

Or more like—a combining of senses. Of becoming one...

It was like a marriage. Both felt it—yet neither could say.

And then they were on the banks of the Yarra, approaching the wide expanse of the river-bank gardens. It was the most gorgeous day and Melbournites were making the most of it. There were couples and families and jugglers and ice-cream vendors and dogs on leads, and…

'Enough,' Shanni decreed. 'This is where we stop—or I'll die of exhaustion.'

So they stopped, and they sank onto the grass, removed their rollerblades, lifted Harry out of his pushchair, nestled him between them and settled in for a late lunch.

Hot dogs. Ice-creams. Soft drink and more soft drink—'Because I'm so dehydrated I could drink a river,' Shanni declared, and then they lay back with the sun warm on their faces and watched the rowers lazily stroking up and down the river.

Or rather, Shanni and Harry watched the rowers. Nick watched Shanni.

'What?' she demanded, catching him at his gazing as she gave the last of her chocolate ice-cream a reluctant farewell lick.

'What do you mean, "what?"'

'You've hardly said a word. You just watch me. Do I have ice-cream on my nose? Did my hot dog leave ketchup? What are you staring at?'

It was impossible to lie. 'Just you,' he told her, and the look in his eyes made her blush from the toes up. Dear heaven…

And silence fell again, but this time the silence was different.

They almost slept, only not quite. Because Harry was too excited and Shanni and Nick were too aware…

As the day wore on they rollerbladed through the Botanic Gardens, feeding the ducks, checking out every nook and cranny, feeling the oneness of themselves as a unit.

And in his pushchair Harry finally slept the sleep of the exhausted.

And the absolutely content.

As evening fell they pushed themselves home, back along the esplanade. Still there was so little to say to each other— but this was no awkward silence. It was as if they hardly knew where to start—as if there was a great well of un- tapped sharing that they were not brave enough to tap for fear of starting a flow that each was somehow fearful of.

The rollerblade hire place was locking up as they reached it. The owner smiled as he saw them come, not angry in the least.

'Now, how did I know you'd be the last of my customers back?' He beamed. 'If I may say so, as I watched the three of you head off this morning it did my old heart good. "See," I said to the wife, "there's still love in the world." ' He nudged his elderly wife and the two of them beamed with such goodwill that Nick nigh on blushed as crimson as Shanni.

'When will your leg get better?' the lady asked Harry, who, having just woken up, was lazily content to lie back and watch the world without fear. Normally a stranger talk- ing to him would have made him shrivel. Not today.

'The doctor says I might have to wear my cast until Christmas,' Harry said. 'But then it'll be all better.'

'You're a lucky little boy.' The lady smiled.

And so did Harry.

'I know,' he said proudly. 'And Shanni's going to sleep with us tonight.'

They left with Nick's face burning, and Shanni in a bub- ble of laughter she couldn't contain.

Then they ate—again!—in a restaurant overlooking the beach—and then...

'What next?' Harry demanded. He'd had a solid after-noon nap and was raring to go.

'Nothing that requires legs.' Shanni groaned. 'I can't feel my feet. They've gone walkabout. Or rollerbout. This af-ternoon my body forgot it was no longer a teenager, but it's remembering now!'

Nick couldn't agree more. He smiled at Shanni—at the pair of them—and he knew what would work.

'Pictures, I think.'

'Pictures?' Harry frowned.

'Have you ever been to the cinema?'

'No.'

'That settles it. Pictures.'

Which wasn't as easy as it sounded. Nick's local cinema catered for adults, and Shanni checked out its main offer-ings and shook her head.

'No chance, Nick Daniels. "Mature audience" doesn't mean three-year-olds.'

'But that means there's only…'

'Yes.' She grinned as they perused the advertisement board. 'There's a choice of exactly one. Or one hundred and one. *101 Dalmatians*, to be precise.'

'*101 Dalmatians*,' Nick said faintly and Shanni chuckled and took his arm. Which felt weird, but very, very good.

'Romance and comedy and dogs,' she said. 'What could be better? And fantasy to boot. It's just what this weekend is all about.'

So Nick sat through a movie he'd never dreamed of see-ing. As a child movies hadn't been for the likes of Nick and, as an adult with his carefully acquired sophistication he'd have died rather than see such a show. But, to his amazement, he found himself chortling along with Shanni and Harry, and gasping as Harry did.

Then, as the dalmatians' deadly peril grew closer and Harry abandoned his seat and clambered onto Nick's knee, it was entirely natural that Shanni should move across to Harry's seat to stay close—and it was also natural that Nick's free arm should come around her shoulders so they could gasp together...

Happily, evil was conquered, and one hundred and one dalmatians were consigned to live happily ever after. And, as Harry, sleepy, sated, and totally content, was carried out into the foyer—it was also natural that Nick's hand should hold Shanni's...

'Nick!'

The exclamation stopped them dead. It was a voice he knew only too well. Nick turned and there was Abe Barry, his head of chambers, heading straight for him. Rachel, Abe's wife of thirty years, was right beside him, and both were smiling their pleasure. 'Nick! What on earth are you doing in town?' Abe demanded. 'How are you, boy?'

'I'm fine, thank you, sir.' Nick adjusted Harry in his arms and extended his hand in greeting. It was pumped enthusiastically, but Abe's eyes were on his companions.

'This is Shanni McDonald, sir,' Nick told him. 'And Harry. They're from Bay Beach.'

'You're settling in well, are you?' Abe's keen eyes missed nothing. His eyes darted from Harry to Shanni and back again. 'Read about that bit of drama in the papers. Damned business. Thought you said nothing would ever happen in Bay Beach.'

'I don't get to try the case.'

'But otherwise...the job's turning out well?' His eyes were still questioning Shanni's presence.

'I...you could say that.' What else was he supposed to say?

'I'm very happy to hear it.' Rachel tucked her arm into her husband's. She inspected Shanni and smiled her pleasure. 'Hello, Nicholas. This is the kindergarten teacher you were held hostage with, isn't it? I saw your picture in the paper. What a dreadful experience. And…Harry, did you say? Is this your little one, dear?'

'He's ours for the weekend.' Shanni smiled and her smile hugged Harry all by itself. 'Aren't we lucky?'

'What film have you been to see?' Abe asked, frowning. This jigsaw didn't quite fit, and he wasn't a man who took kindly to gaps. 'Rachel dragged me along to see some fine-art film. Did you see that?'

'No, sir. We saw *101 Dalmatians*.'

'*101 Dalmatians*…' He stared, confused. This wasn't the Nick he knew. 'Have we seen that, Rachel?'

'Yes, dear,' she said placidly. 'With the grandchildren last school holidays.'

'Oh.' The elderly man's bushy eyebrows beetled down, astounded. 'So we did.' And Nick practically groaned. He could see this story being all around the lawcourts within the week.

But…

'Don't you worry, my dear, I won't let him gossip,' Rachel said conspiratorially, and started pressing her husband away. 'Not yet, anyway. I can tell that things are too precious and too new to breathe about. All the best, my dears. Nick, I'm so excited for you. I've worried about you so dreadfully…'

And she led Abe off—speechless.

And so was Nick.

'I…we should go home. It's time for bed,' Shanni said finally, fighting mounting colour. 'I mean…'

Her colour rose higher.

'I know what you mean,' Nick managed. 'And, yes, I entirely agree with you. It's time to go home.'

There was no trouble getting Harry to sleep. No trouble at all! He hugged them both, put his head onto the pillow and was out like a light before Shanni and Nick could move from the bed.

And then what?

Nick didn't know. This was unfamiliar territory.

Nick was so aware of Shanni's body beside him he could hardly breathe, and he was so tense! Why, on earth? Shanni was just a woman. A country kindergarten teacher. There was no reason at all why every nerve in his body should be screaming its awareness of her.

But it was—and she seemed to sense it.

'I'm tired too,' she said, awkwardly, it seemed, and she stood on tiptoes and gently kissed him—lightly on the cheek, as one would kiss a friend. 'I'm going to bed. Good-night, Nick.'

And she took herself off to his spare room fast, leaving Nick with the overwhelming impression that she was escaping.

Which she was. There wasn't much sleep where Shanni was going. Shanni lay in the unfamiliar bed and stared at the ceiling. She had absolutely no idea what was going on here. Or… Maybe she did and she was just running scared.

She knew nothing about this man, she told herself desperately. He was totally out of her ken.

She liked country boys—boys who had family, who liked kids, dogs, horses, country things. She had a very clear idea of where her life was going, and it didn't include someone like Nick Daniels.

'He wears designer suits,' she whispered into the night.

But he wasn't wearing one now.

She almost wished he was. It'd make it easier. She shouldn't be so attracted.

Why not?

Because he was damaged goods! she told herself—and there was another puzzle. Why did he seem like that? She lay with her hands linked behind her head and tried to figure it out.

Damaged? Most women wouldn't see it, she thought. They'd see the exterior. They'd see Nick's almost breath-taking good looks. The wealth and position. His great smile and the sophisticated lifestyle....

They were all things that didn't interest her in the least.

Or maybe... Maybe she was a liar. Maybe the smile was important. The way he let his guard down when she least expected it and the way he grinned down at Harry as if they were co-conspirators.

Which they were. Co-conspirators in pain, she thought, wondering just how different their backgrounds were. If they were the same, Nick would never let her close now. For Harry, aged three, there was time to heal, but a man in his thirties, who'd been taught the hard way never to let anyone close, was a different proposition entirely.

What was happening this weekend was miracle enough, she told herself fiercely, and she mustn't expect more. If Nick could give a part of himself to help heal a child who needed him, that was all she should ask.

But there was a part of her that was screaming for more—demanding more. It wanted a part of him for herself. There was a part of Shanni that wanted Nick's love, and it would be content with nothing less.

'Which is just stupid,' she said savagely into the night. 'You'll just break your heart down that road, Shanni McDonald, so you might as well forget about it. Right now!'

And Nick?

Just through the wall Nick's thoughts were as jumbled as Shanni's.

Some things, though, were crystal-clear. He knew ex-actly what his body was telling him. He wanted Shanni like a physical ache, and that ache was almost unbearable. He wanted her, and he wanted her, and he *wanted* her. All day he'd wanted her. Every time she brushed his arm—in the cinema his need had driven him nuts—every touch and every look and every faint scent of her was driving him to distraction.

But…she was a country girl. She'd have certain expectations he had no hope of meeting. What he wanted, he decided, was to make fierce, passionate love to her—to get this need out of his system.

But she wasn't his normal type of woman. He knew instinctively that she wasn't a girl who'd accept a one-night stand.

And afterwards, if he succeeded in making love to her and she felt committed, no matter how plain he made it that he wanted no ongoing commitment, he had to live in the same town as her for another two years. Her sister was his clerk of courts. Her brother was one of the policemen he worked with.

Like it or not, he was Bay Beach's magistrate, and he knew that making casual love to Shanni would mess that up like nothing else could.

So seduction? No. Out of the question.

Which shouldn't faze him, he told himself into the bleak darkness while Harry slept on contentedly beside him. There were women he'd been attracted to in the past who were unobtainable. He'd never found it a problem; he'd simply moved on to someone else who'd accepted him on his terms. Seducing country innocents wasn't his style.

This nearness to Shanni was only for this night, he told himself. For one night he had to keep himself under control and then get on with life.

Move on to someone more suitable.

But… He wanted Shanni!

*   *   *

'No!'

The scream spilt the night, terror knifing through every last corner of the apartment and Shanni's feet were out of bed and onto the floor almost before she'd heard it. What...

'No, no, no. Don't hit me. Don't...'

She was out of bed, diving through to the next-door bedroom with the speed of light, shoving open Nick's door and flicking on the switch so she could see.

No one was hitting anyone. Of course not.

Nightmares!

Harry was sitting bolt upright in bed, his face ashen and his eyes staring at some invisible spectre as if it was the most fiendish apparition imaginable. Nick was with him— holding the boy tight but making no impression on the little one's terror. He looked up as Shanni entered, and his face was almost as white as Harry's.

'He started struggling in his sleep. Sobbing. And now this... Dear God...'

'No!'

The scream was heart-rending. Harry's terror was raw and real, and Shanni's heart clenched in horror at what must have gone on in the past to cause this.

But this was now. There was no room for delving into the past. Nick's attempts at comfort weren't working. This fear had to be faced and worked through.

And this was no time for gentle soothing.

She crossed to the bed, sat down facing Harry and took his rigid little hands in hers, forcing him to turn in Nick's arms to face her.

Then she spoke, her voice strong and sure and authoritative. 'Harry!' It was a stern command—a voice to be obeyed. 'Wake up, Harry. You're having a bad dream. Can you see me? Harry?'

He didn't focus. The spectre was still there, no matter how tight Nick held him.

'Harry, look at me. Look at me now!' It was her best commanding kindergarten-teacher voice, and finally it seemed to get through. Her face was inches from his. She was right in his line of vision—putting herself between Harry and his terror while Nick held on for all he was worth. It was all he could do.

'Harry, look at me, please. It's Shanni. I'm here with you, and Nick's holding you. We're your friends and we're here. No one's hitting you. Harry, wake up and *look*!'

And finally his gaze moved. It shifted just fractionally, but, instead of an unseeing gaze into distant fear, he focussed waveringly on Shanni.

The terror was still right behind her. She could almost see it, and she had to dispel it. Send it back from wherever it had come from.

'There's no one here but Nick and me. No one else. You're having a bad dream. That's all it is. A bad dream, Harry. No one is hurting you.'

Still the sense of disbelief.

'Nick's holding you and he loves you,' Shanni said strongly. 'Nick won't let anyone hurt you. Will you, Nick?'

'No way.' It was a low growl but it was almost a choke, and Shanni glanced at Nick and saw all sorts of emotions playing on his face.

There were shadows there—but that had to wait until later. Focus on Harry.

'You're with me and Nick. Harry, you have Nick and you have me and you have Wendy. We all love you, and we won't let anyone hurt you. Ever. Do you hear me?'

Nick's hold on his rigid little body tightened even more. Harry was now staring straight at Shanni, a trickle of sweat running down his forehead, and Shanni gave an involuntary shiver.

'It's gone, Harry,' she said softly, holding his hands and not letting her eyes leave his, forcing him to keep looking

at her. 'We're with you. You're safe. Nick and I are right
here. You're with grown-ups who love you. There's nothing to be afraid of.'

'I...' It was a wavering sob.

'Nothing will touch you while you're with us,' Shanni
said gently, flicking an upward glance at Nick. 'I promise.
That's what we're here for. To keep you safe.'

And—slowly—almost unbelievably—Harry nodded.
Shanni saw his body slacken within Nick's grasp, the awful
rigidity fading with the terror.

And then—instantly—his little body slumped against
Nick, his eyes closed and he slipped back into the safety
of sleep, leaving Nick holding him as if he'd never let him
go.

It took three of four minutes before either of them
moved. Shanni was aware that she was shaking. She was
warm enough—she was wearing very non-sexy long flannelette pyjamas—but Harry's terror had left its shadows. It
was still real and palpable in her heart.

She looked at Nick, and she knew he felt the same. And
then some.

'He's safely asleep,' she whispered at last. 'He hardly
woke up. Just long enough to be reassured. He probably
won't remember any of this tomorrow.'

'I couldn't get through to him,' Nick said, shaken to the
core. 'I tried.'

'It's a trick you learn in kindergarten training,' she said.
'Never be gentle with a terrified child. Be direct. Bossy,
even.'

He gave the ghost of a grin. 'You were certainly that.'

'Ask my family. Bossiness is my speciality.' She rose,
resplendent in her pink pyjamas with woolly sheep all over
them, and Nick blinked at the vision she created. Amazing!
'I guess...I'll go back to bed now,' she said. 'If you slip

him down under the covers it's my guess he'll keep right on sleeping.'

'Yes.' Nick looked down at Harry's mop of unruly fair hair, and his mouth twisted into a grimace. There was a part of him that really didn't want to let him go, Shanni thought as she watched. Ever...

He'd been hurt himself, she knew, and she was starting to figure out how badly. Nick had been down this road before, and maybe there hadn't been a Shanni or a Nick or a Wendy for him.

'He's been hit in the past.'

'Yes.'

'Were you beaten as a child?' she asked—and waited.

For a long minute she thought he wouldn't answer. This was a closet that had long been locked, she guessed, never to be reopened, and here she was probing where it hurt most. But if the closet stayed locked, what was inside could well stay there for ever.

'I don't...' He stopped, as if he didn't know what else he could possibly say. Instead he did as Shanni suggested, letting Harry slip down onto the pillows. He adjusted his covers, touched his hair lightly with his strong fingers and then turned to face Shanni.

This was ridiculous. He was wearing boxer shorts—nothing else—and he was bare-chested and felt naked. And she was rumpled from sleep, her curls flying everywhere, and she was standing before him in those ridiculous sheepish pyjamas.

And suddenly he had to tell her. He had to tell *someone.*

No. He had to tell *her.* Explain why it was impossible for him to love.

'Yes,' he said harshly. 'I was beaten. Badly. The last time...'

'The last time?'

'The last time my mother decided she wanted me. My

stepfather didn't. He gave me a pretty bad time before I was taken away.'

How old were you then?

'Seven.'

It was as much as he could say, but she needed to know no more.

'Nick...'

'Don't you dare feel sorry for me,' he said roughly—more roughly than he'd intended. 'That was twenty-five years ago, and if I'm not over it now I never will be.'

'I don't think you can ever be over something like that.'

'Like being mistreated? Lots of kids are.'

'Like not being loved,' she whispered. 'Kids can bounce back from a bad time—but if they don't think they're loved...'

'Harry'll be okay.'

She hadn't been talking about Harry—but now she turned to look down at the little boy, following Nick's gaze. Even though the king-sized bed had been split into two, Harry's share of the bed still seemed absurdly large for one so small.

'I guess...' she smiled and turned back to Nick '...if you stay on his side...'

'Hey, I'm committing myself to nothing here,'

'You've already committed,' she told him. 'You know it. It's scaring you stupid, but you can no sooner walk away from him now than you could fly.'

'I can't adopt him.' Heck, what was she saying?

'I know that. Harry knows that.' Her smile softened, and suddenly her hands came out and took his. 'But it doesn't stop either of us from knowing that you're committed to loving him. Right up to here.' She did her tiptoes thing again—but this time she reached up and kissed him on the forehead.

'And we think you're just wonderful.' Her voice was

husky with emotion. 'A vote's been taken, Magistrate Daniels. The court's come to a verdict, and the verdict is fantastic.'

It was a gamble, and she knew exactly what she was doing. Shanni stood absolutely still, her hands still holding Nick's, and her heart seemed to stop beating. The whole world seemed to hold its breath.

She'd laid her heart on the line here, she thought dazedly. She could do no more than that. Nick might not want commitment but he had it—right here in his hands.

And he stared down at her with his dark, fathomless eyes, and she knew that his heart was torn, just as hers was.

But hers had come to a decision.

'Nick,' she whispered, and her heart reached out for him. 'Nick, love…'

'Shanni…'

It was too much. She stood in his grasp, in her absurd pyjamas with her heart on her sleeve and all the love and compassion and care in the world right there in her eyes.

A man would have to be inhuman to resist something so lovely. So utterly, wonderfully desirable.

This was not sensible. But nothing tonight was sensible.

With a groan that felt almost like the breaking of chains, Nick took her into his arms and kissed her.

CHAPTER NINE

SHANNI had been kissed before. Many times. Starting from when she was about twelve or maybe even before. Mary had been right when she'd told Nick the McDonald girls were desirable and boys were interested from the time they could walk. So she knew what to expect. Or she thought she did. What she got was—different.

It was Nick.

She'd felt this force fleetingly, in the car the night they'd mock-kissed outside the farmhouse, but not like this. This was like a zillion volts charging right through her, starting somewhere about her toes, coursing straight through from her lips, into Nick's body and back to her again.

This was…right. This was how it should be, she thought wonderingly. It was as if their worlds had been heading along two different paths until this moment, but now the paths had converged. Ended. Reached their destination and their destiny.

This was where she was meant to be. Shanni's awareness of anything but this man had shut down entirely. There was only Nick, and her whole body was lighting up as if it was on fire.

Nothing like this had happened to her before. She couldn't believe she felt like this, and he felt it too. He must. Somehow…she knew.

Nick's hands were holding her body into his, pulling her up to meet his kiss, and she could feel the rough maleness of his chest beneath her breasts. Her hands felt the naked expanse of his back and she clung—and clung and clung.

Nick…

Nick!

Dear heaven, she wanted him. Her thighs were on fire. Her whole body was on fire. There was a white-hot melt starting somewhere in the region of her heart.

Who knew where it had come from? How it had started? Who knew?

Maybe it had begun with attraction and compassion and the fact that Nick was a man and Shanni was a woman and he was funny and gorgeous and like no one she'd ever met before. But now... It wasn't like that now.

It was as if they were cleaved together. Like magnet to metal—two forces irresistibly linked with a force neither had recognised until this kiss.

Nick!

But... *Harry was in the bed behind them!*

The little boy was fast-asleep, night terrors gone. There was little chance he would wake now—but he was there, and he was in the only part of consciousness she was capable of raising.

Nick was aware of him, too. Almost as soon as the thought of responsibilities entered her mind, the thought was with him as well. He needed to say nothing. She could feel it.

She *knew* this man, and together they could not forget the little one. Never.

So he put her away from him—just fractionally, but the force it took was unimaginable and the link remained, unbroken.

'One moment... Not here. But...Shanni, love, wait.'

He moved swiftly to the bedside-drawer and she knew what he was fetching—knew it and gloried in it, because this was right. Now! Now was right.

And then he was back, sweeping her up to lie in his arms, his eyes caressing her, making love to her without a single sound. Then he turned to Harry's bed.

For a moment they gazed down together at the sleeping child, ensuring his sleep was as sound as they knew it must be. Their need for each other was urgent, but not so urgent they could forget how much this little boy needed them.

But Harry needed nothing. His face was calmly peaceful, almost smiling, and Shanni's mouth curved into a smile to match. It was the smile of one who knew what it was to be loved.

'He won't wake,' she whispered, and it was a proclamation of love all by itself.

And then, silently, they left the room. Nick carried her into the adjoining room where the big bed waited, and he left the doors ajar so they could hear Harry if he woke.

As Shanni had known Nick would. She knew this man so well. She was so close to him.

And she wanted to be closer.

'My love...'

'Hush.' Nick's dark eyes gleamed down at her, desire flaring. It was too late to draw back now, and both of them knew it. It was too late for separation.

Shanni's bed was before them, the covers thrown back from when she'd left with such haste. Nick laid down his precious burden and then stood, looking down at her in the dim light cast from the street lights outside.

And all the love and desire and the longing in the world were in that look, Shanni thought lovingly. A man hungering for what he'd thought he could never have.

She raised her hands, pleading.

'Come to bed, my love,' she whispered. 'Come to me...'

But with a superhuman effort he held back, and heaven knew how. 'Shanni...' Somehow he made his voice work, and, again, heaven only knew the effort it cost him. 'Are you sure?'

Was she sure? How could he ask that question? How could she not be sure?

This was her man. Nick was her love and nothing had ever felt so right in her life before.

'I love you, Nick Daniels,' she said, and her eyes gently teased him. 'I loved you even when you wore your horrid tie and I thought you were nothing but a city lawyer on the make—and that's saying something. But now I can run my fingers through your hair and you're a country magistrate who belongs with me, begorra.' She twinkled up at him but her smile was pleading. 'And you're the most desirable man I've ever met in my life before. If only you'll come closer…'

'Shanni…'

'Get down here, Nick Daniels.' She seized his hands and pulled him down to her, and he was so stunned he almost fell. Full-length he came to her, his naked chest crushing her breasts under her crazy pyjamas and his body stiffening with desire as her fingers came up and raked through his unruly hair…

With such tenderness he thought he'd melt with wanting her.

Dear God, he was on fire.

And so was she.

'Love me,' she whispered in the night. 'Nick, love me— now.'

It wasn't Nick doing the seduction. She wanted him as badly as he wanted her, and there was no possibility he could pull back.

The consequences of this night would just have to wait until tomorrow.

For tonight, there was only Shanni.

But no matter how long the night—or how wonderful— there was always the morning. The dawn saw Nick wide awake, staring up at the ceiling as if it had betrayed him.

By his side, Shanni slept on. His arm was around her,

holding her close, and her nakedness and her warmth were still arousing him as no woman had ever aroused him in his life.

He thought she was the most beautiful, the most desirable, the most wonderful being he had ever met.

But he felt...wrong. Trapped?

She must have sensed it. Somehow... Her eyes flew open, she smiled at him with that smile he knew and loved so much it hurt, and her fingers came up to trace the furrow between his brows.

'My love... Nick, what is it?'

The knowledge had been with him all night—not mentioned until now. But it was time to speak and it had to be said.

'You didn't tell me it was your first time,' he said heavily, and her eyes widened.

'No.' She thought it over, still sleepy with love and warmth and happiness. 'I didn't. Does it matter?'

'Yes.'

She smiled again and shrugged. This was nonsense. 'I can't see why.'

'Shanni, you've been engaged. I thought...'

'You thought what? And I *have not* been engaged!' That woke her. She pushed herself up on one elbow and glared down at him in mock indignation. 'Are you saying there's something wrong with me because I didn't sleep with *John*?' There was such revulsion in her voice that he almost grinned.

'No, but...'

'But what?'

'Why me?' he said, and she stared down at him, her smile fading. The echo of his trouble shadowed her face.

And what could she say? There was only room for the truth. What was between them was too wonderful for anything less. 'I guess…I guess I wanted it to be special. The first time…'

'And?'

'And it was.' But her smile was now uncertain. 'For you, too?'

'Of course. But Shanni…'

'I know it's not your first time.' She smiled, teasing him. 'Or I assumed. Unless you've been saving your condom just for me for all these years…'

'Shanni…'

'I'm not fussed.' She turned within his hold and kissed him lightly on the mouth—and his need for her rose so strongly within that it was almost overpowering. 'What's past is past.'

Only it wasn't. His past was always with him.

'I'm not what you want,' he said heavily.

Silence. Then… 'What exactly is it that you think I want, Nick Daniels?' Her voice was low—husky—and somehow there was a hint of anger in it. 'Apart from you making love to me.'

'I don't know.' His arm tightened around her shoulders, involuntarily, catching her to him again. 'Husband material, maybe?'

The anger was definitely there. She hauled herself out of his arms, sat up in bed and glared at him for all she was worth.

'You're kidding. You think I'll be expecting to *marry* you now—just because I've slept with you?'

Yeah. Maybe he did think that. He blinked, flummoxed, but she was still on her soapbox.

'Just because I wanted it to be special doesn't mean I wanted it to be *that* special! So you can take that look of a trapped dodo right out of your eyes—this minute! And make love to me again.'

'I…'

'Are you refusing?'

'No.' Hell, no! 'But...'

'Stop thinking, my lovely Nicholas,' she ordered. 'Men are always dangerous when they think. I said I love you and I do, but loving you doesn't mean I'm setting any trap. I'm taking each moment as it comes, and so should you. So shut up, lie back and think of England. Do anything but think!'

Only, of course he did think.

He made love to her as if there was no tomorrow, and at the back of his mind he knew just how desperately he was falling in love with this lady. She'd said she loved him and the words had exposed a hunger he hadn't known he was capable of. But...could he return it? Could he forge a tomorrow for them? He loved her, sure, but to be a part of a family...

They showered—together—and dressed and were waiting respectably when Harry woke. And still Nick thought...

They took Harry to the zoo—and decided meerkats were the most wonderful animals in the world—and they laughed at the seals and gawked at giraffes and ate popcorn and lay on the lawns and soaked up the sun—and all the while Nick thought.

Could he take this further? If so, how far? She was so wonderful. This was so wonderful.

Could he let himself fall...?

He had his whole life mapped out, and Shanni wasn't in it, but suddenly his life plans were looking pretty bleak. Shanni, on the other hand, was looking more desirable by the minute. She lay on her back on the grass and ate her ice-cream cone upside down—'A feat I've been practising for a zillion years,' she said—and she chuckled with Harry and told Nick he was *soooo* boring for choosing vanilla and choosing to eat his ice-cream the right way up.

And she found a T-shirt with a meerkat printed on the front—and promptly bought an extra-large one for Nick and a very small one for Harry and insisted Harry and Nick put them on immediately.

So Nick was forced to buy her one too—of course—and they walked around the zoo in three matching, ridiculous meerkat shirts—and then Nick saw a sign asking for sponsors to adopt a meerkat, and they promptly adopted one called Tim, because he had a sore foot and he was Harry's favourite.

'His birthday's next month,' the keeper told them. 'You'll come to celebrate?'

'We surely will,' Shanni said, eyes glowing, and Nick knew that, expectations or not, he was in so deep now he just might never get out. And he didn't know if he wanted to get out.

And then they caught the last train home, and life started again. Life as it was meant to be...

'Shanni, I'm engaged. Shanni, Shanni, Shanni...' It was Louise, the next McDonald sister down from Shanni. She was standing on the platform waiting for them, and she was fairly bursting with excitement and news. She hugged Shanni, she hugged Harry and then, for good measure, she hugged Nick as well.

'I came to collect you myself because I wanted to tell you first and Aunt Adele hasn't been answering her phone all weekend. Where have you been? No matter. Shanni, Alastair asked me to marry him on Friday night, just after you left. Of course I said yes. We've been celebrating all weekend and there's a party happening at home right now. So you need to come right on out.'

Shanni looked helplessly at Nick—this was just what she didn't need! But Nick just shrugged and smiled. He'd been growing more and more quiet on the train journey—and now this!

'Go ahead,' he told her. 'It's been a great weekend. My car's here. I'll take Harry home.'

It was a dismissal—kindly meant, but a dismissal for all that—and Shanni's heart sank.

'Hey, you need to come, too,' Louise told him, but Nick shook his head.

'No. It's a family party.'

'But…'

'Let him be, Louise,' Shanni said shortly, fixing her sister with a look she couldn't ignore. She sighed, trying to take her mind off the expression on Nick's face—the look that said he was back to formality. 'By the way, Louise—did you know that Aunt Adele has never been better in her life? That the story of her illness was a ruse to get me to Melbourne?'

'Oh…' Louise had the grace to blush. 'Well, sort of. It was Mary's idea, though.'

'Why?' Shanni was *so* aware of Nick's expression. Blankly smiling… It was as if he was restoring himself to someone she thought had disappeared. But he hadn't. He was now remembering who he was.

Any minute now he'd put his blasted tie back on!

But Louise had regained her composure and was unabashed. She gave Shanni a cheeky grin. 'McDonald matchmaking, of course,' she said blithely. 'Plus Mary thought you needed to get away, Shanni, and we thought you three might have fun. Did you?'

'Yes, but…'

'There you go, then.' All was right in Louise's world and she had no intention of letting a guilty conscience get in the way of her joy. She beamed at the three of them. 'Should Alastair ask Nick to be a groomsman to match you as my bridesmaid?'

'No,' Shanni said, revolted. 'Louise, don't be stupid.'

But Louise was incorrigible. 'Am I being stupid, Nick?' she demanded, and peeped a smile at him. Nick managed a smile back as he lifted Harry into his arms and prepared to carry him out to the car park.

'I don't think I'm groomsman material,' he said shortly.

'How about groom itself?'

'Louise, butt *out*!' Shanni was practically speechless with mortification. Her family was impossible...

'I guess I'm not that either,' Nick told her, and he gave Shanni a smile that was as impersonal as it was gorgeous. It was a smile that said the world was to be greeted with friendliness but held at arm's length.

'Goodbye, Shanni,' he said. 'Enjoy the party. Harry and I need to go. We'll see you around.'

We'll see you around... The words echoed forlornly around the empty railway station and even Louise's smile faded.

'Shanni, I'll be at kindergarten tomorrow,' Harry said urgently from his safe haven of Nick's arms. He was trying to keep his precious link with the two of them for as long as possible. 'And don't forget Tim Meerkat's birthday.'

'I won't forget,' Shanni said, and she gave Harry a hug— and Nick was sort of included somewhere in the hug because, after all, he was holding Harry. 'Tim's a part of our family. We've adopted him—so how can we possibly forget?'

But Nick said nothing. Shanni gave him one long, searching look as her heart sank still further—and then she turned and followed her sister.

Because Nick's face told her she wasn't welcome to follow him.

He was nuts.

Nick settled Harry back with Wendy, promised him he'd

visit on Tuesday night and again on Thursday, left him excitedly telling Wendy all about his new friend, Tim Meerkat, and then tried to drive home.

He couldn't. He physically couldn't turn the wheels of his car toward the courthouse.

Shanni was with her family, and there was a huge part of him that wanted to be right there. Part of the McDonald clan.

Part of a family.

But if he took this next step then he knew he couldn't walk away. As he could no longer walk away from Harry.

Shanni...

The car slowed. He'd been automatically steering toward the farm, but now he turned off onto the coast road. Neither way, then. Not home and not to Shanni.

This was tearing him in two, he thought bitterly—to separate from Shanni now—but how could he take this next step?

It scared him stupid.

He couldn't just leave it there, he knew. Her face at the railway station had been shocked into stillness. She'd taken it without flinching, but he knew he'd hurt her.

Of course you've hurt her, he told himself savagely. You made love to her. And now...now she needs commitment. She deserves nothing less.

As she was committed.

She'd let him take her to him, he thought—she'd let him love her, and all the love in the world had been written clearly in her eyes. Sure, she'd said she didn't intend him to take things further, but Nick was no fool, and somehow he knew her as he knew himself.

Or maybe more so. Maybe he couldn't know himself as he knew Shanni, and that was one of the reasons he loved her. Shanni had no ghosts in her past to rise and haunt him.

No shadows that screamed *Keep your distance*—commitment was a thing to be feared at all costs.

So he steered his car onto the headland and sat for hours staring straight out to sea—and staring right within himself, searching deeper than he'd ever looked before.

If he let himself take the love Shanni had to offer...

He'd be taking and taking and taking, he told himself bitterly. What could he offer a girl like this? He had no family, he had no deep well of love; he had only his own insecurities and needs.

And one of those needs—cultivated from the time he'd been able to recognise any world at all—was the need to hold himself apart.

If he drove out to the McDonalds' home now, he'd be welcomed with open arms, he knew, and he also knew he'd feel so claustrophobic he'd want to run. Because they'd expect things of him. Expect him to open his heart as Shanni had opened hers.

No!

He'd hurt her already, he told himself. Hurt her maybe unforgivably. But if he didn't intend to take this loving further, then the time to move on was right now.

But... Dear heaven, he had to tell her.

'Shanni.'

The hubbub was fading. Her family were still in party mode, but Louise and Mary were talking bridal plans, the men were out on the verandah talking 'men's talk'—or getting away from talk of veils and guest lists—and the younger McDonalds were drifting reluctantly toward bed. Shanni was inclined to join them. Her mother had been eyeing her with concern for a good while now, but Shanni had deflected her nicely. Sort of.

She knew her mother couldn't be deflected for ever.

'*Shanni...*' It was fifteen-year-old Hatty calling from the hall. 'It's your gorgeous magistrate on the phone,' she yelled, and the remaining hubbub died immediately.

All eyes flew to Shanni.

Her colour mounted. Drat her family. Drat them all... Nick must have heard that yell—he could have heard it in the next county at the level Hatty yelled.

It's your gorgeous magistrate on the phone...

There was nothing for it. With the eyes of her entire family following her, Shanni went to talk to her gorgeous magistrate.

'Shanni...'

And as soon as she heard his voice she knew what he intended saying. She'd known it from the railway station but until this minute she'd hoped...she'd sort of hoped...

She'd desperately hoped!

'Nick...'

'Shanni, I'm sorry...'

She turned her back to the kitchen, blocking her family out entirely. 'Nick, can we talk? Privately?' It was an urgent plea but she knew already what he'd say.

'There's no point.'

'Nick...'

'I've behaved like a rat,' he said heavily. 'I should never have let you come near me. To just...take you...'

'We both wanted it,' she said steadily. 'I wanted it as much as you.'

'I can't take this any further,' he told her, and Shanni heard the pain in his voice and she wanted to slam the receiver down before the words were uttered. She knew what he was going to say, but she couldn't stop him. And here it came.

'You're a wonderful woman,' he said softly. 'Magic. Shanni, you deserve better than me.'

'You don't think I could be the judge of that?' She was

fighting with everything she had. There was no room for pride here. There was only her love.

'Shanni, I've been alone for a long time now.'

'Too long.'

'Maybe. But…it's what I'm accustomed to.'

'But not because it's what you want. You're afraid to be anything else.'

'Yes,' he said honestly. 'That's the truth, Shanni. But that's who I am.'

'You won't walk away from Harry?' Her voice rose, fear flooding through for the child, and when he answered she sagged against the passage wall in some sort of relief.

'No, Shanni. I won't do that. While Harry needs me I'll be there for him.'

'And…if I need you?' She tried so hard to keep her voice strong—but there was raw pain coming through and Nick must have heard it. His breath was raw with jagged need— a need he couldn't acknowledge even to himself.

'I…I don't think you can,' he said at last. 'I think…needing me is really, really stupid thing. Because there's nothing I can give.'

And, after that, there was nothing more to do than to get on with their lives.

Apart.

CHAPTER TEN

NICK spent the next four weeks throwing himself into work as he'd never worked in his life before.

He rearranged the courthouse. He set up a new filing system. He put in a new computer and sat up until after midnight every night entering data as if it was vital the thing was up and running a week ago last Friday.

He ignored the mayoral ball and suffered the consequences—especially since at least twelve people told him that Shanni had been there and had looked lovely and had danced all night....

His court cases became protracted. He didn't miss a legal point and the local lawyers and police sighed and cut back their lunch-breaks and wondered how long this could last.

'Because you might want to drive yourself to an early grave but I don't see why you should take the rest of us with you,' Mary said darkly. 'Just because you've messed up your love life...'

'I have not messed up my love life,' Nick retorted, throwing his gown aside after a torrid little traffic case that he'd managed to stretch out to two hours of court time. 'You know nothing of my personal life and that's the way I like it.'

'That's the way you like it? Ha!'

'You don't know...'

'Hey, I'm a sister to the other side of the equation,' she told him. 'I can see both sides. So I see you trying to fill every available minute with work and I see Shanni going around with dark shadows under her eyes like she hasn't slept for a week.'

Ouch. That hurt.

It couldn't matter. She'd just have to get over it, Nick told himself savagely, and she seemed to be trying hard enough. And it was better to hurt her now than later as he tried to mould himself into something he could never be.

A family man.

'You love her, you know,' Mary said conversationally, watching his face. 'Why not give in and admit it?'

He had. That was just the problem. He'd admitted that fact to himself and then some. He did love her, and if he didn't love her he wouldn't be so darned scared of hurting her.

And he wouldn't know how much she deserved someone better.

There was still Harry.

Harry was his saving grace—his time of peace. With Harry, he'd made his commitment. He was forced to spend time with him—forced to take every evening he could and head to Wendy's to read him a bedtime story, or take him to the beach after work, or walk along the cliff tops, hand in hand, a peaceful silence between them.

It was a weird relationship. Nick knew Wendy was watching it with satisfaction and it perturbed him—he felt her expectations of him were unjustified—but Harry took him at face value and asked nothing more than that he'd be there for him.

He was content to give that much, and the less Harry asked of him, the more he found he was prepared to give. As the weeks wore on, he found himself automatically walking down to the children's home each evening—because Harry's face would light up when he saw him. If he didn't arrive, there was no recrimination the next night, but Harry's pleasure was intensified.

And so was the pleasure for Nick. To his astonishment he found himself thinking about the little boy during the day—figuring out what they could do that evening—wandering past the book store, hesitating and then going in to choose a story...

Different stuff. Not like Nick Daniels at all...

It helped fill the ache left by Shanni. The ache of knowing what he was missing.

But it didn't fill it completely. Nothing could fill that void, but he was accepting that the darkness of his void was there for ever.

'You've achieved a miracle.'

It was four weeks after the Melbourne trip. Four weeks after Shanni... Nick had finished reading Harry his bedtime story and had emerged to find Wendy alone. For once she wasn't surrounded by children. She motioned to the coffee pot, waited until he was settled and then repeated herself.

'What you've done for Harry, Nick...well, it is like a miracle.'

'I've done nothing.'

'Nonsense. You've given him a friend.'

'He's been one to me.' It was true, and it gave Nick a shock to hear himself say it. A friend...

He wasn't into friends. Or...not friends like Harry. Not friends he loved.

'Then maybe Harry's done as much for you as you have for him,' Wendy said gently, and watched his face.

'I don't know what you mean.'

'I mean...until now you've been as solitary as Harry. You don't need to be, you know. It's simply a matter of letting go. Releasing a part of you and trusting it to someone you love.'

And suddenly they weren't talking about Harry.

Or maybe they were. The feelings she was talking of... It was crazy. Entrusting part of him to Harry... He'd never do that.

But as he sat there, with Wendy's calm eyes resting on

him, making him think, he knew suddenly that he was wrong to believe he could never do it. Because…somehow he'd done it already. He'd given a part of himself to a child.

The thought was like a lightning bolt. Until now he hadn't been involved at all. Not one whit. He'd so carefully cut himself free of all ties, but now, with Harry, he was involved, whether he liked it or not.

And with Shanni…

It was fear, he thought suddenly. That was what was driving him. Up until now he'd figured it was consideration for Shanni that was hauling him back—worry that he'd hurt her more than he had already. Maybe it was—partly—but it was more than that.

If he took the next step to loving and something happened…

He wasn't ready. He was scared.

'Hey, Nick.' Wendy's hand came over his, warm and reassuring. 'There's no need to have angst over this. Take this one step at a time. You've given Harry so much. Don't push yourself.'

'Shanni…'

'I guess Shanni knows you need space,' she said gently. 'And maybe she's prepared to wait.'

He shook his head. 'That's stupid. I'm not…'

'Not ready to talk about it? That's fine by me.' She lifted his empty mug from his hands and moved across to the sink. And then her shoulders stiffened, as if she was bracing herself for something unpleasant. 'But we do need to talk about Harry.'

'Harry?' He stared. 'Why?'

'We think he's ready for fostering.'

'Fostering?'

'He can't stay here long-term,' Wendy told him, turning back to face him, trouble in her eyes. 'This is a temporary refuge for troubled and orphaned kids. It's not a stable home and that's what Harry desperately needs. He's been here too long already.' She sat again, facing him with eyes that were suddenly sad. It was as if she knew that Nick's need was almost as great as Harry's, but the little boy must come first.

'We have a couple who are willing to take Harry on as a long-term foster-child,' she told him gently. 'Maybe they'll even adopt him if it turns out okay. Normally if a child is available for adoption we like to do it straight away, but in Harry's case we've hesitated. As you know, we didn't consider him ready. But now...'

'Yes?' Why was his world suddenly bleak.

'We're still not sure if he'll handle adoption. We suspect he won't, straight off. He distrusts the world, and he needs space. But he trusts you now, he trusts you totally, and if you were to keep the link...'

'How do you mean?'

'I mean, if we move him to local foster-parents and you keep visiting...then slowly back off. Not so much as he'll notice straight away, but just gradually cut back...so that in two years when you return to the city he's not bereft. He'll have parents by then, and hopefully they'll have taken your place and more.'

'It sounds good to me,' Nick said, trying to keep his voice light. Trying really hard...

Because it didn't sound good at all. His void was becoming a sickening chasm of emptiness.

'A few weeks ago I'd practically given up on this happening,' Wendy told him. 'I can't believe the change you've wrought. But now he's content and he's socialising and Harry's social worker believes we need to move fast before he becomes too established. Too fond of me.'

'And of me?' Nick's eyes met hers, steady and questioning, and Wendy nodded.

'Yes.'

'And...is it supposed to hurt?' He closed his eyes. He couldn't believe the pain. 'Does it hurt you?'

'That's what my job is,' she said, striving for lightness. 'I'm accustomed to this. Take them in, love them to bits while they're here, but then launch them out to their own families.' She smiled. 'I'm accustomed now. Almost. And I have the rest of the kids to worry about. For you, though...'

'I don't need anyone else.'

'No?' She smiled and cocked an eyebrow and he knew she didn't believe him.

Change the subject. It was the only thing he could do. 'When will this happen?'

'As soon as possible,' she said heavily. 'Maybe Monday. Tomorrow's Sunday. I'll talk him through it and...'

'If he objects?'

'He's three years old,' Wendy told him. 'We don't give him a choice. I know, at the moment, Harry wants to stay in this place—with you and with me—but we're not his long-term parents, Nick. So we need to stand aside now and let those who can love do their best.'

It was the right thing—the sensible decision—a path that would give Harry a chance at this lottery called life.

Just...why did it feel so darned bleak?

And, going out, Nick met Shanni coming in.

She stopped dead at the gate as he walked out through the door. Her smile slipped and then was carefully repinned.

'Nick,' she said, smiling again, and there might well have been nothing between them at all. If he hadn't seen that tiny slip... 'You've been visiting Harry?'

'Yes. Of course. I promised.'

'Great.' It was almost sarcastic, and the pain in her voice made him flinch. She stood aside so he could pass, and he should have kept right on going. Instead he paused. He couldn't help himself.

'Harry's asleep,' he said, and he sounded inane, even to himself.

'I'm not here to see Harry,' she told him. 'Wendy's my friend, and it's Wendy I've come to see. She's upset.'

'Upset?' He frowned. He hadn't seen it. 'Why?'

'You're not stupid, Nick. Because of losing Harry, of course.'

His frown deepened. 'I don't understand.'

'She's told you about the arrangements for fostering?'

'Yes, but I thought... She's happy with the arrangements. It's the right thing.'

'You don't think she'll miss Harry? After almost a year of trying to get through to him?'

'I thought...'

'That she's tough? Don't you believe it. She bleeds just like the rest of us.'

'This is her job, Shanni.'

'Yes.' Shanni nodded, her eyes bleak. 'It is, but there's not many who could do it. Wendy gives and gives some more. She takes in children, battered and bruised and from all sorts of backgrounds, she loves them, she fights to get through to them, and then, when she sees they're on their way to healing—when they're just at the point where they can love her—she sends them off to long-term carers. She sends them away.'

He thought this one through and saw it. Saw Wendy's need for the first time, instead of just his own. 'I guess it must hurt at that. So...why does she do it?' he asked slowly. 'Open herself to hurt like that?'

'She has courage.' Shanni's voice tried to be light but it didn't quite come off. 'She knows she's the only chance these kids have of finding love. By hurting herself she gives them that hope.'

'I hadn't seen...'

'No,' she said bleakly, and for the first time she allowed her own hurt to show. 'You don't see, do you, Nick? You don't see there are others in the world who are just as fearful as you—but who have the courage to open themselves to love.'

'I...'

'Goodnight, Nick. Leave others to care. You just look after yourself!'

And how could he sleep after that?

Nick spent the night staring at the ceiling and thinking of every option under the sun. And, as dawn came, he knew what he must do.

He wasn't one of these people who could love and risk losing all. He had no place here. Shanni had been right when she'd implied he had no courage. He didn't. He was a coward and he knew it.

So...there was nothing for it but to stop hurting people and get back to the city where he belonged.

Forget the ambition. It wasn't so important any more. Maybe facelessness and solitude were more important than a position as high-court judge.

But Harry still needed him.

So he'd come at the weekends to visit Harry while he was needed, he told himself. That was all. On Monday he'd hand in his resignation. He'd give a month's notice and he was out of here.

For good!

His intention stayed with him for all of the next morning. He stayed inside and tried to focus on legal journals but the pages danced before his eyes, meaningless and empty.

Wendy would be telling Harry about his new family, he

thought. Maybe his new mum and dad would be visiting. How would he be taking it?

Who could know what the little boy would make of it? Wendy, though…Wendy would be hurting.

And somewhere Shanni would be aching for all of them. Enfolding them all in her huge heart and taking their pain into her. The three of them whirled through his thoughts and gave him no peace.

Harry. Wendy.

Shanni…

He was going nuts!

He was leaving.

That afternoon he walked for miles, but it didn't help one bit. When he got back, the answering machine told him he had messages waiting, and the phone rang again as he walked in the door. For some reason, as he lifted the receiver, he had a sudden lurch of dread.…

'Nick?'

'Shanni…' He didn't need more than one syllable to know she was in trouble. Something was dreadfully wrong.

So much for not caring. Ha! His heart twisted in fear. 'Shanni, what is it?'

'Harry's not with you?'

'No. Why should he be?'

'Dear, God… Nick, he's run away. Wendy told him about the foster-parents and he took it on the chin—you know, like he does—not saying anything but just looking straight ahead. But looking like he's blind. She said that Helen and Doug, his new prospective parents, were coming to see him this afternoon. That was all. Then one of the other children grazed her knee. Wendy took her into the bathroom to clean her up and when she finished he wasn't there.'

'Then, where…?'

'That's just it, we don't know,' Shanni said raggedly. 'Nick, we've all looked. Everyone's looking. We've been trying to contact you for hours but I knew you wouldn't have him without telling Wendy. The police are here now—Rob—everyone. Oh, Nick...'

Her breathing was way too fast, as if she'd been running. 'Nick, does Harry know where you live? Have you ever taken him to your place above the courthouse? We thought that was where he'd try to go.'

'No.' Nick frowned, trying to make his fearful mind focus. There'd never been a need to bring him here.

'Have you told him where you live?'

'I don't think so.' His brow creased in concentration, thinking it through. 'No.'

'We've looked everywhere.' Silence—and then he heard her breath draw in from shock. As if she'd just had a dreadful thought. 'No!'

'What?'

You remember that day in the kindergarten after the hostage thing. You told him where you lived.'

'I didn't.'

'You told him you lived on Borrowah Mountain,' she said raggedly. 'Nick, Harry can see Borrowah from his bedroom window. We've searched every street in town—every inch of the beach. But if he's headed for the mountain... It's not so far to the start of the National Park. Nick, he could be in thick bush by now. Dear God...'

CHAPTER ELEVEN

THEY searched for the rest of that day, and then for one of the longest nights Nick had ever known. Every able-bodied person in town and for miles around the district turned out to scour the mountainside, and Nick searched with them.

Shanni was asked to stay at base camp in case he returned, as Wendy couldn't leave her other charges, but the look on her face told Nick it was one of the hardest things she had ever done in her life. To stay still and wait...

At least he could search, and Nick searched like a man possessed, but it was like looking for a needle in a haystack. One tiny crippled boy in rugged national park bushland, some of it so thickly forested that it took machetes and raw strength to hack a man's way through.

Why had he ever said it? Nick demanded of himself over and over again as he bashed through the bush. Why had he ever told Harry he lived in such a dreadful place?

Shanni must hate him. But she couldn't hate him for it as much as he hated himself, he thought bleakly. He was hating himself enough for the both of them.

All through that long night, as he joined the line of searchers bashing their way in lines through the forest, Nick was calling himself every type of fool he could think of. Why had he told the child he lived in one of the most inaccessible places in the state?

Because he'd wanted to be inaccessible, he acknowledged, and that need for solitude was now exacting such a cost he couldn't bear it.

And...for what? A solitude he no longer craved. He was

no longer independent, he acknowledged. His very self now depended on the welfare of one small boy.

And one woman.

When he'd turned up at search headquarters—a mobile police caravan set up in a clearing at the base of the mountain—he'd looked at Shanni's face and he'd seen a terror matching his own reflected in her eyes. For some reason Harry had spun his little self around her heart, becoming as much a part of her as he was part of him. If they couldn't find him...

Please... Please...

The same pain in Shanni's eyes was reflected in others... The policemen organising search teams. Team members. All Shanni's family. The older children from the children's homes associated with Bay Beach orphanage. Shopkeepers, mill workers, teachers, boy scouts, even the women's lawn bowls association, for heaven's sake.

The lady bowlers were making cups of tea as if their lives depended on it and the fitter ladies were donning protective clothing instead of bowling whites and bashing through the bush with the best of them.

Every last person in the district was desperate to help, and Nick's distress was reflected in their faces. One little boy's pain, taken on by so many...

'Any man's death diminishes me...'

These people knew what it was to care, but that care came at a cost. A cost Nick was prepared to pay, and more. He'd pay anything it took. Harry...

But, in the enforced breaks the search coordinators forced him to take, it was Shanni's face he kept coming back to. There was raw agony in her eyes and he felt such a twisting knot of helplessness and rage and fear that he didn't know how to hold it in. How could he face her after such stupidity?

Dear God, how could he bear it? He had to have some-one to hold—and he was alone.

Because that was the way he wanted it?

No! At two in the morning his group was called in after the moon went behind clouds, and he felt so sick he wanted to retch. He lifted his hand and smashed it down on a tree stump, and then gazed helplessly at the graze he'd made on his skin.

These people…they knew how to care and he didn't. He'd told a baby that he lived on Borrowah Mountain…

He closed his eyes in despair—and then opened them at the feel of someone touching him gently on his injured hand. Shanni…

'Nick?' It was a tentative whisper and the look he gave her was bleaker than death.

What could he say to her? He'd caused this hurt.

'You don't need to speak to me,' he told her.

'That's nonsense. We need each other.'

'Shanni, how could I have done it?' he demanded, his voice raw with despair. 'How could I have done something so criminally stupid? I must have been mad.'

'You weren't to know it could ever come to this,' she said softly, and then, before he could say anything more, she wrapped her arms around him and held him. And held him and held him, as if her life depended on it.

And for one long moment he kept himself ramrod-stiff. It needed only this. He didn't deserve comfort! That she should try and comfort him when he was so dreadfully at fault…

'We'll find him,' she said softly. 'I know we will. Nick, he's here somewhere. You're not to blame yourself. You're here now for him, and together…we'll find him. Please…'

And she held him close, kissing him softly on the hair, holding him like a child and pouring her love into him. She was willing into him a strength that, alone, he could never have.

And when they moved away—inches, but enough—there was a new, steely determination between them that was an affirmation that the whole was far greater than the parts. Together they could face this, feeding each other strength.

'We can find him,' Shanni said. 'We must. Together we must.'

'He won't come out.' Heaven knew what made him see it, but suddenly he knew. This thing that he felt—that Shanni had given him. Trust. Love. Completeness. It gave him knowledge.

Harry was his child as surely now as Shanni was his woman. And Harry trusted Nick.

Things were suddenly blindingly clear. There was no chance of these searchers finding Harry—not if one small boy didn't want to be found—because Harry was heading for Nick with the same single-minded purpose that Nick would feel if Shanni or Harry was in danger. He was heading for the one person in the world he trusted and he loved.

Wendy had told him new people were coming to see him—people he didn't know but who wanted to be his parents. So Harry had run, and he'd keep running. He wouldn't want to be found by anyone but Nick.

All night Harry must have been trying to find Nick, but if he'd come to this point, where the road ended and the wilderness of mountain started, he would have gone nowhere but up.

His leg was so weak—so damaged. He couldn't climb strongly. In the dark he must have stumbled and fallen over and over. He'd be terrified.

But if he heard people searching—calling, as each group had been—would he answer? No, Nick thought, seeing things with a clarity that he hadn't seen before. Harry was terrified of more than the dark. People hadn't treated him with love. They were things to be feared.

But not Nick. Whether he deserved it or not, Harry loved Nick.

The thought made Nick's heart wrench so hard it must surely break.

'Let's try this another way,' he said strongly, turning to the men who were coordinating the search parties. When the moon had gone behind clouds they'd called in all but the most experienced searchers until dawn. Now Nick looked again at Shanni, seeking confirmation in her eyes, but he knew he was right. 'At dawn…let me go up. With Shanni. No one else.'

'You'd be lost in minutes up there, sir,' a coordinator told him, shaking his head. The head of the emergency services was hard and efficient, and the last thing he wanted was an extended search if the town's magistrate got himself lost.

Nick thought this through. Of course they were right. He was city born and bred and, no matter how much he wanted it otherwise, he didn't know the bush.

'Then stay with us, but behind,' Nick said. 'Stay silent and let me call, without anyone else making a noise. It's my guess he'll be hiding. I should have thought this through before, but if he'll come for anyone, he'll come for me.'

The search coordinator looked at Shanni. He knew her. She was a local. One of them. 'Is that right, ma'am?'

And Shanni was looking at Nick with eyes that were clear and steady. The terror had receded. Her mind was back in gear.

As Nick had thought—the parts were stronger than the whole. She'd gained strength with their love.

'If Harry wants to be found by anyone, he wants to be found by Nick,' she said, her own thoughts crystallising. 'I think…I think Nick's right. He's Harry's only chance. And, because Nick doesn't know the bush, he'll also be able to see the path Harry might take—not looking at the overall picture, like you and me, but at the logical way for a three-year-old. And, please, God, he just might do it.'

So, at dawn, the mass of searchers were held back—'We'll give you 'til noon, sir'—and one small group of experienced bushwalkers were equipped to the hilt to accompany them. But they let Nick decide the course.

'I'm going straight up,' Nick told them. 'Bear with me. I'm a dope in the climbing department, but then so's Harry. So every time there's a decision I'm going to ask myself what Harry would have done. And I'm going to yell myself hoarse.'

He took Shanni's hand in his hand and held it. Hard.

'Ready, my love?' The endearment slipped out unnoticed, but it was between them, anyway. Acknowledged for ever, whatever this day held. They were no longer two. They were a man and a woman made one, in need and in love.

'I'm ready,' she said. She gripped him as if she couldn't bear to let go, and then she turned back to the searchers who had to stay behind but who were breaking their hearts to help.

'We'll bring him back.'

'Please…'

'Nick will do it.' She looked at him, her eyes calm and clear and determined. 'I know it. He loves Harry.'

And three hours and twenty minutes later, hoarse from calling and over five hundred yards, as the crow flies, straight up the mountain, Nick called for the thousandth time and thought he heard a faint response.

He stopped dead. The tension in Shanni's hand was tangible—dear God, please...

The group behind them also stopped. They'd heard it, then. It wasn't just him.

'Harry!' Nick's voice echoed out around the mountainside and he and Shanni moved in the direction he thought the sound had come from. The rest of the group surged behind them, two of the searchers cutting a path but dropping back as soon as it was clear.

'Harry, it's Nick. Harry...' He didn't let Shanni go—not for a moment. 'Harry, I'm here. Harry...'

And thirty seconds later they rounded an outcrop and stopped.

Harry was crouched motionless in the midst of a massive prickly grevillea that was three times as big as he was. The bush had been in the way of up. He'd tried to crawl over it, the thorns had stuck from all sides and he'd slipped through and was wedged fast.

'Harry!' With a great shout of joy, Nick released Shanni's hand and clambered up, ignoring thorns, ignoring pain, reaching the tiny, battered and scratched little boy and gathering him to his heart as if he'd never let him go again.

As he never would.

And somehow Shanni reached them, too, and they were sitting in the middle of the dreadful thorns and clinging together—three and yet one—and Shanni was weeping and so was Nick, but they were together and Nick knew this was how it was going to be.

For ever.

'I thought you lived here.'

The team had got them down from their mound of thorns but were standing back in joyous silence, savouring success and letting them be. Harry was so exhausted he was limp in Nick's hold, but his arms still somehow clung. His eyes devoured him. 'I thought you lived up here all by yourself. So I came.'

'I don't live here, Harry.' Nick's voice was a hoarse whisper—he could still hardly believe he had the child in his arms.

'Not any more?'

'No.' Nick had his face in Harry's hair, but his eyes, over Harry's head, were watching Shanni. Watching the love on her face. The tears. The joy.

The destiny.

'Then, where do you live?' It was an exhausted whisper, but he was still desperate to know. And Nick knew why he was desperate. It was because Harry didn't believe in happy endings. He needed to know in case he was torn away again and had to find his Nick.

So this time Nick knew what the answer had to be. The only answer.

'I live with you,' he said strongly, hugging him close. 'From today, Harry. From today, I live with you. And with Shanni, if she'll have me.'

'Shanni…' Harry twisted his face around to see and she was right there, all the love in the world shining from her eyes.

'Wendy told you you needed a mummy and a daddy—right?' Nick asked, and he looked at Shanni again and saw her watching Harry—with such a look—and his heart twisted with such love that he didn't think he could bear it.

'Mmm.'

'How would you feel if that was Shanni and me? If we were your mummy and daddy.'

Harry stiffened in Nick's hold. He pushed his head back and gazed into Nick's face, searching. This little one had been told lies before.

'You'd be my daddy?'

Heck, all he wanted was to burst into tears. Instead he made his voice gruff and deep and magistrate-like. Definite.

'If you want me. That's what I want. More than anything in the world.'

'Why?'

There it was. The simple question—with the simple answer.

'Because I love you,' Nick said strongly, and his spare arm came out and held Shanni to him as well. She hugged him back—hugged both of them—her eyes glistening with tears and all the love she possessed shining in her face.

'Because I love you and I love Shanni,' he said. 'I love you both with all my heart. And I figure…if I'm to come down from my mountain, what better reason could a man have than that—to come down for love?'

It was mid-afternoon.

Harry had been checked over medically, had been pronounced one very lucky young man; his scratches and bruises had been anointed; he'd been fed, cuddled, put to bed and cuddled some more until he'd fallen fast asleep from sheer exhaustion.

It was his last sleep in this bed, Nick had told him. When he woke they'd move his belongings to where he belonged. With Nick.

And now Wendy was watching over him one last time, her joy tinged with sadness. 'I'm getting too old for this,' she said as she watched Nick and Shanni cluck over their little one. 'It's time I moved on. Maybe took a chance at permanent fostering.'

'Loving and letting go isn't something you can do for ever,' Shanni said softly, watching her friend's face, and Nick could only agree.

Loving and letting go? No! He'd only just learned to love, and he intended to hold.

Somehow he forced himself to focus on Wendy. 'Can you do that? Move to permanent fostering?' he asked, and Wendy nodded.

'Soon.' She smiled as one of her charges peeped in, holding up a scratched finger for inspection and sympathy. She beckoned her in, lifted the little girl and hugged her hard, then turned back to gaze down at Harry. 'Some children have the capacity to break you up. But now and then there's a happy ending that makes it fine. Like you and Shanni and Harry... Go on, you two. Go and sort out your future while I watch over your baby.'

And she stayed with Harry and watched as Nick led Shanni outside.

They didn't speak. As if of one accord they made their way to Nick's car and Nick drove the short way to the beach. He stopped the motor and for a long moment sat looking out to sea.

Shanni sat silent. She knew exactly what was happening. Nick was saying goodbye to something he'd never wanted in the past but he'd learned to guard as if it was the most important thing in the world. And now...he was saying farewell to solitude for ever.

And then he turned to Shanni. His love.

His face was tense, she thought. Unsure of what was to come.

'Shanni, when I said back there...to Harry...that we...' he faltered.

Her heart lurched. No! Maybe she was wrong. Maybe, even now, he wanted to back away.

'I know, Nick,' she said heavily. 'You didn't mean it. Or if you did...' She fingered her hands. 'Being Harry's parents...Nick, I'm not staying with you just for Harry.'

'I wouldn't ask you to do that.'

She turned to him then, tilting her chin, a trace of the redoubtable Shanni returning.

'What would you be asking, then, Nick Daniels?'

And the answer was there, already written. Clear as day, only he'd been too blind to see it. Until this day.

'I'm asking you to marry me because I love you more than life itself,' he said. 'You've given yourself to me with all the love in your heart and I was too blind, too stupid and too cowardly to return it. But I need it, Shanni. I need your love like I've never needed anything so much in my life. You're part of me. You and Harry...

'Me—and Harry?'

'Could you bear to be a part of a family?' he said simply. 'My family?'

'You and me and Harry?' There was a glimmer of laughter in her lovely eyes and she held out her hands and took his between them. 'Oh, Nick...Nick, that's all I want in the whole wide world. You and me and Harry... Oh, my love...'

And then, as he took her into his arms and kissed her and the afternoon sunshine exploded in a mist of joy and love and desire, Nick thought that life could hold no more than it possibly did at this very moment.

He was loved, and he loved in return. He'd reached the pinnacle...

But his love was pulling out of his arms, and the laughter was still there.

'Me and you and Harry?'

'Mmm.'

'It's not enough.'

What was she talking about? Love?

'I think we should get this straight,' she said, trying for sternness but her voice was husky with love. 'Before we commit.'

'Aren't we committed?'

'I want this legal.'

'As legal as you want. I'll sign anything.' He paused, his legal training screaming all sorts of warnings. Drat his legal training! For this moment he was a lover—not a magistrate. 'What do you want me to sign?'

She chuckled, a lovely carefree sound that echoed around them as an affirmation of their love. Of their passing from dark to light...

'I want two dogs and a horse written into the contract.'

'Two dogs and a horse...'

'And four more children. At least.'

'Four...'

'And Wendy and her foster-kids must be welcome whenever they want to stay with us.'

'Is this a marriage we're arranging—or a menagerie?'

'Both.' She laughed into his eyes, he smiled back, and she knew she needed no legal agreement. She knew she had him in the palm of her hand.

'Okay, Your Worship, that about sums it up,' she said sweetly. 'Do you still want to be a high court judge, by the way?'

'I can't see two dogs, one horse, five kids, plus assorted hangers-on in my city apartment. How long did you say your last judge stayed in this town?'

'Thirty years,' she said serenely.

'Thirty years...' He took her into his arms and they might well have been married right at that moment. No vows could ever be more permanent than this. 'Thirty years, eh? It seems to me...'

'What does it seem, my lovely Nicholas?'

'It seems to me like thirty years is not nearly long enough.'

It's hard to resist the lure of the Australian Outback

One of Harlequin Romance's best-loved Australian authors

Margaret Way

brings you

Legends of the
OUTBACK

Look for

A WIFE AT KIMBARA (#3595)
March 2000

THE BRIDESMAID'S WEDDING (#3607)
June 2000

THE ENGLISH BRIDE (#3619)
September 2000

Available at your favorite retail outlet.

NEARLYWEDS

Almost at the altar—
will these *nearly*weds
become *newly*weds?

Harlequin Romance® is delighted to invite
you to some special weddings! Yet these are
no ordinary weddings. Our beautiful brides
and gorgeous grooms only *nearly* make it
to the altar—before fate intervenes.

But the story doesn't end there....
Find out what happens in these
tantalizingly emotional novels!

Authors to look out for include:

**Leigh Michaels—The Bridal Swap
Liz Fielding—His Runaway Bride
Janelle Denison—The Wedding Secret
Renee Roszel—Finally a Groom
Caroline Anderson—The Impetuous Bride**

Available wherever Harlequin books are sold.

HARLEQUIN®
Makes any time special ™

MAITLAND MATERNITY

Where the luckiest babies are born!

In May 2001 look for

GUARDING CAMILLE
by Judy Christenberry

**He promised to watch over her—
day and night....**

Jake Maitland, FBI agent and black sheep of the Maitland
clan, had finally come home. And he had a whole lot
of trouble on his tail....

Camille Eckart was Jake's latest assignment. He'd been
chosen as her protector, to keep her safe from her mobster
ex-husband. Only, little did he guess that Camille's main
objective was to make Jake see her not as a case,
but as a woman....

Silhouette®
Where love comes alive™

HARLEQUIN®
Makes any time special ™